"You're a great guy, but I'd prefer to keep things between us professional," Kayla said.

"So no more kisses?"

"No more." She had to hold back a sigh. The kiss really had been great, but kissing Dylan again would only lead to more kissing and hugging and caressing and... She shoved the thoughts away and sat up straighter. They were almost to the turnoff for her house.

He switched on his blinker to make the left turn. Behind them, headlights glowed in the distance. Kayla squinted and shielded her eyes from the glare in the side mirror. What was the guy behind them doing with his brights up? And he was driving awfully fast, wasn't he?

Dylan took his foot off the brake, prepared to make the turn. But before he could act, the car behind them slammed into them, clipping the back bumper and sending the cruiser spinning off the road and into the ditch. The air bags exploded, pressing Kayla back against the seat. Then she heard another sound—the metallic popping of bullets striking metal as someone fired into their vehicle.

MURDER IN BLACK CANYON

Cindi Myers

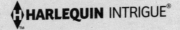

HARLEQUIN INTRIGUE®

For Coco—Female PI Extraordinaire

Recycling programs
for this product may
not exist in your area.

ISBN-13: 978-1-335-72104-4

Murder in Black Canyon

Copyright © 2017 by Cynthia Myers

Printed in U.S.A.

www.Harlequin.com

Cindi Myers is the author of more than fifty novels. When she's not crafting new romance plots, she enjoys skiing, gardening, cooking, crafting and daydreaming. A lover of small-town life, she lives with her husband and two spoiled dogs in the Colorado mountains.

Books by Cindi Myers

Harlequin Intrigue

The Ranger Brigade: Family Secrets

Murder in Black Canyon

The Men of Search Team Seven

Colorado Crime Scene
Lawman on the Hunt
Christmas Kidnapping
PhD Protector

The Ranger Brigade

The Guardian
Lawman Protection
Colorado Bodyguard
Black Canyon Conspiracy

Rocky Mountain Revenge
Rocky Mountain Rescue

Visit the Author Profile page at Harlequin.com for more titles.

CAST OF CHARACTERS

Dylan Holt—The newest member of the Ranger Brigade has returned to his hometown to help his parents run the family ranch. He can't understand why young people are leaving their real families to live with a so-called prophet in the wilderness. He wants to prove to Kayla that she can depend on him, but she's resistant.

Kayla Larimer—The private detective has tracked down a senator's wayward daughter to a group camped in the wilderness. She knows a con when she sees one. She doesn't trust anyone, including Dylan.

Daniel Metwater—Son of a wealthy industrialist, Metwater has forsaken his upbringing to preach peace and love to a wandering band of followers who are camping on public land. He calls himself a prophet, but the Ranger Brigade believes he's hiding a bigger secret—maybe even murder.

Special Agent Frank Asher—An FBI agent on personal leave who is found murdered outside Daniel Metwater's camp. Had he come to the camp to speak to his former lover, Andi Matheson—or was he conducting his own investigation into Metwater's background, and asking the wrong questions got him killed?

Andi Matheson—The wealthy socialite is Daniel Metwater's most ardent follower, having joined the group after she learned Frank Asher was married. Pregnant with Asher's child, is she angry enough over his deception to have murdered him?

Senator Pete Matheson—The senator hired Kayla to find Andi, but now that she's been located, he's disappeared. Is his disappearance related to Asher's death?

Chapter One

As jobs went, this one paid more than most, Kayla reminded herself as she parked her battered Subaru at the mouth of the canyon a few miles from the Gunnison River. A private investigator in the small town of Montrose, Colorado, couldn't be overly picky if she wanted to keep putting food on the table and paying rent, though interceding in family squabbles had to be right up there with photographing philanderers on her list of least-favorite jobs.

Still, this assignment gave her an excuse to get out into the beautiful backcountry near Black Canyon of the Gunnison National Park called Dead Horse Canyon. She retrieved a small day pack from the backseat of the car and slipped it on, then added a ball cap to shade her face from the intense summer sun. A faint dirt trail marked the way into the canyon, through a windswept landscape of dark green piñon and juniper, and the earth tones of sand and gravel and scattered boulders.

A bird called from somewhere in the canyon

ahead, the high, trilling call echoing off the rock and sending a shiver up Kayla's spine. Maybe she should have brought a weapon with her, but she didn't like to carry the handgun, even though she was licensed to do so. Her work as a private investigator seldom brought her into contact with anyone really threatening. She spent most of her time surveilling cheating spouses, doing background checks for businesses and serving the occasional subpoena. Talking to a twenty-four-year-old woman who had decided to camp out in the desert with a bunch of wandering hippies hadn't struck Kayla as particularly threatening.

But that was before she had visited this place, so isolated and desolate, far from any kind of help or authority. Someone holed up out here could probably get away with almost anything and not be caught. The thought unnerved her more than she liked to admit.

Shaking her head, she hit the button to lock her car and pocketed her keys. The hard part of the job was over—she had tracked down Andi Matheson, wayward adult daughter of Senator Peter Matheson. Now all she had to do was deliver the senator's message to the young woman. Whether Andi decided to mend fences with her father was none of Kayla's business.

Her boots crunched on fine gravel as she set out walking on the well-defined path. Clearly, a lot of feet had trod this trail recently. The group that referred to themselves as simply "the Family" had a permit to camp on this stretch of public land outside the national park boundaries. They had the area to themselves. No one else wanted to be so far away from things like electricity, running water and paved roads. Her investigation hadn't turned up much information about the group—only some blog posts by the leader, a young man whose real name was Daniel Metwater, but who went by the title of Prophet. He preached a touchy-feely brand of peace, love and living off the land that reminded Kayla of stuff she'd seen in movies about sixties-era flower children. Misguided and irresponsible, maybe, but probably harmless.

"Halt. You're not authorized to enter this area."

Heart in her throat, Kayla stared at the large man who blocked the path ahead. He had seemingly appeared out of nowhere, but he must have been waiting in the cluster of car-sized boulders to the left of the path. He wore baggy camouflage trousers and a green-and-black camouflage-patterned T-shirt stretched over broad shoulders. His full beard and long brown hair made him look like a cross between a biker and an old-testament patriarch. He wasn't armed, unless you counted the bulging muscles of his biceps, and what might have been a knife in the sheath on his belt. She forced herself to stand tall and look him in the eye. "This is public land," she said. "Anyone can hike here."

"We have permission to camp here," Camo-man said. "You'll need to walk around our camp. We don't welcome gawkers."

What are you hiding that you don't want me to see? Kayla thought, every sense sharpened. "I'm not here to gawk," she said. "I came to visit one of your—" What exactly did she call Andi—a disciple? A member? "A woman who's with you," she decided. "Andi Matheson."

"No one is here by that name." The man's eyes revealed as much as a mannequin's, blank as an unplugged television screen.

"I have information that she is. Or she was until as recently as yesterday, when I saw her with some other members of your group in Montrose." The three women, including Andi, had been leaving a coin operated Laundromat when Kayla had spotted them, but they had ignored her cries to wait and driven off. She had been on foot and unable to follow them.

"We do not have anyone here by that name," the man repeated.

So maybe she had changed her name and went by Moon Flower or something equally charming and silly. "I don't know what she's calling herself this week, but she's here and I want to talk to her," Kayla said. "Or satisfy myself that she isn't here."

She spread her hands wide in a universal gesture of harmlessness. "All I want to do is talk to her. Then I'll leave, I promise. What you do out here is your business—though I'm pretty sure blocking access to public land, whether you have a permit or not, is illegal. It might even get your permit revoked." She gave him a hard look to go with her soft words, letting him know she was perfectly willing to make trouble if she needed to.

He hesitated a moment, then nodded. "I'll need to search you for weapons. We don't allow instruments of destruction into our haven of peace."

She was impressed he could deliver such a line with a straight face. "So that knife on your belt doesn't count?"

He put a hand to the sheath at his side. "This is a ceremonial piece, not a weapon."

Uh-huh. And she had a "ceremonial" Smith & Wesson back at her home office. But no point arguing with him. "I'm not armed," she said. "And you'll just have to take my word for it, because I'm not in the habit of allowing strange men to grope me, and if you lay a hand on me I promise I *will* file assault charges." Not to mention she knew a few self-defense moves that would put him in the dirt on his butt.

A little more life came into the man's face at her words, but instead of arguing with her, he turned and walked down the trail. She followed him, curious as to what kind of compound the group had managed to erect in the wilderness.

The man turned into what looked like a dry wash, circled a dense line of trees and emerged in a clearing where a motley collection of travel trailers, RVs, pickup trucks, cars, tents, tarps and other makeshift shelters spread out over about an acre. To Kayla, it looked like a cross between the Girl Scout Jamboree she had attended as a child and the homeless encampments she had seen in Denver.

No one paid any attention to her arrival. A dozen or more men and women, and half as many children, wandered among the vehicles and shelters, tending campfires, carrying babies and talking. One man sat cross-legged in front of a van, playing a wooden flute, while two others kicked a soccer ball back and forth.

Kayla spotted Andi with a group of other women by a campfire. She looked just like the picture the senator had given her—straight blond hair to the middle of her back, heart-shaped face, upturned nose and brilliant blue eyes. She wore a long gauze skirt and a tank top, her slim arms tanned golden from the sun, and she was smiling. Not the picture of the troubled young woman the senator had painted. Rather, she looked like a model in an advertisement for a line of breezy summer fashions, or for a particularly refreshing wine.

Kayla started across the compound toward the

young woman. Camo-man stepped forward as if to intercept her, but her hard stare stopped him. "Andi?" she called. "Andi Matheson?"

The young woman turned toward Kayla, her smile never faltering. "I'm sorry, but I don't go by that name anymore," she said. "I'm Asteria now."

Asteria? Kayla congratulated herself on not wincing. "My name's Kayla," she said.

"Do I know you?" Andi/Asteria wrinkled her perfect forehead a fraction of an inch.

"No. Your father asked me to check on you." Kayla stopped in front of the woman and scrutinized her more closely, already mentally composing her report to the senator. No bruises. Clear eyes and skin. No weight loss. If anything, she looked a little plumper than in the photos the senator had provided. In fact…her gaze settled on the rounded bump at the waistband of the skirt. "You're pregnant," she blurted.

Andi rubbed one hand across her belly. "My father didn't tell you? I'm not surprised, but he did know. It's one of the reasons I left. I didn't want to raise my child in his corrupt world."

Interesting that the senator had left out this little detail about his daughter. "He was concerned enough about you to hire me to find you and ask you to get in touch with him," Kayla said.

Andi's smile was gone now. "He just wants to try to talk me into getting rid of the baby." She turned to the two women with her. "My father can't understand the happiness and contentment I've found here with the Prophet and the Family. He's too mired in his materialistic, power-hungry world to see the truth."

Dressed similarly to Andi, the other two women stared at Kayla with open hostility. So much for peace and love, Kayla thought.

Andi turned back to Kayla. "How did you find me? I didn't tell anyone in my old life where I was going."

"I talked to your friend Tessa Madigan. She told me about attending a speech Daniel Metwater gave in Denver, and how taken you were with him and his followers. From there it wasn't that difficult to confirm you had joined the group."

"I only want to be left alone," Andi said. "I'm not harming anyone here."

Kayla looked around the compound, aware that pretty much everyone else there had stopped what they were doing to focus on the little exchange around the campfire. Even the flute player had lowered his instrument. Camo-man, however, had disappeared, perhaps slunk back to guard duty on the trail. "This isn't exactly a garden spot." She turned back to Andi. "What about the Family attracted you so much?" Senator Matheson was a wealthy man, and his only daughter had been a big part of his lavish lifestyle until a few months ago. Kayla had found dozens of pictures online of Andi and her father at celebrity parties and charity benefits, always dressed in designer gowns and dripping with jewels.

"The Family is a real family," Andi said. "We truly care for one another. The Prophet reminds us all to focus on the things in life that are really important and fulfilling and meaningful. Satisfaction isn't to be found in material wealth, but in living in harmony with nature and focusing on our spiritual well-being."

"You can't live on air and spiritual thoughts," Kayla said. "How do you all support yourselves?"

"We don't need a lot of money," Andi said. "The Prophet provides for us."

Camping on public land was free and they didn't have any utility bills, but they weren't living on wild game and desert plants, either—not judging by the smell of onions and celery emanating from a pot over the fire. "You're telling me your Prophet is footing the bill to feed and clothe all of you?"

"I am blessed to be able to share my worldly goods with my followers."

The voice that spoke was deep, smooth as chocolate and commanding as any Shakespearean actor. Kayla turned slowly and studied the man striding toward them. Sunlight haloed his figure like a spotlight, burnishing his muscular, bare chest and glinting on his loose, white linen trousers. He had brown curly hair glinting with gold, dark brows, lively eyes, a straight nose and sensuous lips. Kayla swore one of the women behind her sighed, and though she had been fully prepared to dislike this so-called "prophet" on sight, she wasn't immune to his masculine charms.

The man was flat-out gorgeous and potentially lethally sexy. No wonder some women followed him around like puppies. "Daniel Metwater, I presume?" Kayla asked.

"I prefer the humble title of Prophet."

Since when was a prophet humble? But Kayla decided not to argue the point. "I'm Kayla Larimer." She offered her hand.

He took it, then bent and pressed his mouth to her palm—a warm, and decidedly unnerving, gesture. Some women might even think it was sexy, but Kayla thought the move too calculated and more than a little creepy. She jerked her hand away and her anger rose. "What's the idea of stationing a guard to challenge visitors to your camp?" she asked. "After all, you are on public land. Land anyone is free to roam."

"We've had trouble with curiosity seekers and a few people who want to harass us," Metwater said. "We have a right to protect ourselves."

"That defense won't get you very far in court if anything goes south," she said.

The smile finally faded. "Our policy is to leave other people alone and we ask that they show us the same courtesy."

One of the few sensible pieces of advice that

Kayla's mother had ever given her was to keep her mouth shut, but Kayla found the temptation to poke at this particularly charming snake to be too much. "If you really are having trouble with people harassing you, you should ask for help from local law enforcement," she said.

"We prefer to solve our own problems, without help from outsiders."

The Mafia probably thought that way, too, but that didn't make them innocent bystanders who never caused a stink, did it?

"I'm not here to stir up trouble," she said. "Andi's father asked me to stop by and make sure she was all right."

"As you can see, Asteria is fine."

Kayla turned back to the young woman, who was gazing at Metwater, all limpid-eyed and adoring. "I assume you have a doctor in town?" she asked. "That you're getting good prenatal care."

"I'm being well cared for," she said, her eyes still locked to Metwater's.

"Asteria is an adult and has a right to live as she chooses," Metwater said. "No one who comes to us is held against his or her will."

Nothing Kayla saw contradicted that, but she just didn't understand the attraction. The place, and this man, gave her the creeps. "Your father would love to hear from you," she told Andi. "And if you need anything, call me." She held out one of her business cards. When the young woman didn't reach for it, Andi shoved it into her hand. "Goodbye," she said, and turned to walk away.

She passed Metwater without looking at him, though the goose bumps that stood out on her skin made her pretty sure he was giving her the evil eye— or a pacifist prophet's version of one. She had made it all the way to the edge of the encampment when raised voices froze her in her tracks. The hue and cry rose not from the camp behind her, but from the trail ahead.

Camo-man appeared around the corner, red-faced and breathless. Behind him came two other men, dragging something heavy between them. Kayla took a few steps toward them and stared in horror at the object on a litter fashioned from a tarp and cut branches. Part of the face was gone, and she was pretty sure all the black stuff with the sticky sheen was blood—but she knew the body of a man when she saw one.

A dead man. And she didn't think he had been dead for very long.

Chapter Two

After ten years away, Lieutenant Dylan Holt had come home. When he had left his family ranch outside Montrose to pursue a career on Colorado's Front Range with the Colorado State Patrol, he had embraced life in the big city, sure he would never look back. Funny how a few years away could change a person's perspective. He hadn't realized how much he had missed the wide-open spaces and more deliberate pace of rural life until he had had the chance to transfer back to his hometown.

It didn't hurt that he was transferring to a multi-agency task force focused on preventing and solving crimes on public lands promised to be the kind of interesting and varied work he had longed for. "For our newer team members, plan on spending a lot of time behind the wheel or even hiking into the backcountry," FBI Captain Graham Ellison, the leader of the Ranger Brigade, addressed the conference room full of officers. "Despite any impression you might have gotten from the media, the majority of our work is routine and boring. You're much more likely to bust a poacher or deal with illegal campers than to encounter a terrorist."

"Don't tell Congress that. They'll take away our increased funding." This quip came from an athletic younger guy with tattooed forearms, Randall Knightbridge. He was one of the Brigade veterans who had been part of a raid that brought down a terrorism organization that had been operating in the area. The case had been very high profile and had resulted in a grant from Homeland Security that allowed the group to expand—and to hire Dylan and two other new recruits, Walt Riley and Ethan Reynolds.

Next to Randall sat Lieutenant Michael Dance, with the Bureau of Land Management, and DEA Agent Marco Cruz. Behind them, Deputy Lance Carpenter from the Montrose Police Department, Simon Woolridge, a computer specialist with Immigration and Customs Enforcement, and Carmen Redhorse, with the Colorado Bureau of Investigation, listened attentively. The veterans had welcomed the rookies to the team with a minimum of good-natured ribbing.

"We do have a couple of areas of special concern," Captain Ellison continued. He picked up a pointer and indicated a spot on a map of the Rangers' territory—the more than thirty thousand acres of Black Canyon of the Gunnison National Park, plus more than 106,000 acres in adjacent Curecanti National Recreation Area and Gunnison Gorge National Conservation Area. "We've got a group camping in Dead Horse Canyon, some sort of back-to-the-land group. Not affiliated with any organized movement that we can identify. They have a legal permit and may be harmless, but let's keep an eye on them."

One of the other new hires, Ethan Reynolds, stuck up his hand. Ellison acknowledged him. "Agent Reynolds has some special training in cults, militia groups and terrorist cells," the captain said. "What can you tell us about this bunch?"

"They call themselves the Family and their leader is Daniel Metwater, son of a man who made a pile in manufacturing plastic bags. He calls himself the Prophet, though he doesn't identify with any organized religion. There are a lot of women and children out at that camp, so it wouldn't hurt to keep an eye open for signs of abuse or neglect. But so far, they've lived up to their reputation as peace-loving isolationists."

"Right." Ellison eyed the rest of them. "We don't have any reason to harass these people, but keep your eyes and ears open. On to other areas of concern…"

The captain continued with a discussion of off-road vehicles trespassing in a roadless area, reports of poaching activity in another area and suspicion of hazardous chemical dumping in a remote watershed.

"Randall, you and Walt check out the chemical dump," the captain ordered. "Carmen, take Ethan with you to look into the roadless violation. Dylan, you go with—"

The door burst open, letting in a gust of hot wind that stirred the papers on the table. "I want to report a body," a woman said.

She was dressed like a hiker, in jeans and boots, a day pack on her back. Her shoulder-length brown hair was in a windblown tangle about her head and her eyes were wide with horror, her face chalk-white. "A dead man," she continued, her voice quavering, but her expression determined. "I think he was shot. Part of his face was gone and there was a lot of blood and—"

"Why don't you sit over here and tell us about it." Carmen Redhorse, the only female on the Ranger team, stepped forward and took the woman's hand. "Let's start with your name."

"Kayla Larimer." The woman accepted the glass of water Carmen pushed into her hands and drained half of it. When she lowered the glass, some of the terror had gone out of her eyes. Hazel eyes, Dylan noted. Gold and green, like some exotic cat's.

"All right, Kayla," Carmen said. "Where did you see this body?"

"I can show you. It's in a canyon on Bureau of Land Management, or BLM, land. The Family is camping there."

"Your family is camping there?"

"Not my family." She gave an impatient shake of

her head. "That hippie group or whatever you want
to call them."

"The peace-loving isolationists," Dylan said.

Kayla looked at him. She wasn't desperate or hys-
terical or any of the other emotions he might have
expected. She looked—angry. At the injustice of the
man's death? At being forced to witness the scene?
He felt a definite *zing* of attraction. He had always
liked puzzles and figuring things out. He wanted to
figure out this not-so-typical woman.

"Are you a member of the Family?" Ethan asked.

"No!" The disdain in her tone dropped the tem-
perature in the room a couple degrees. She slid a
hand into the pocket of her jeans and pulled out a
business card. "I'm a private detective."

"What were you doing in Dead Horse Canyon?"
Graham Ellison asked.

She took another drink of water, then set the glass
aside. "A client of mine has a daughter who cut off
contact with him. He hired me to find her, and I located her living with the group. Then he asked me
to check on her and make sure she was okay, and to
ask her to get in touch with him."

"He had to hire a PI for that?" Dylan asked.

That hot, angry gaze again. "He hired me to find
her, first. He didn't know where she was. After I located her, he thought she might listen to me if I approached her initially."

"Most parents wouldn't be too thrilled about their

kid running off to join a group some people might see as a cult," Ethan said.

"Exactly." Kayla nodded. "Anyway, I found the young woman, gave her the message from her father and was leaving when three men rushed into the camp, shouting. Two of them were dragging a body behind them. The body of a man. He was covered in blood and…" Her lips trembled, but she pressed them together, her nostrils flaring as she inhaled. "Part of his head was gone."

"What were they shouting?" Graham asked.

"They said they were walking out in the desert and saw him lying there."

"Saw him lying where?" Carmen asked.

Kayla shook her head. "I don't know. And before you ask, I don't know why they thought they needed to bring him back to the camp. I told the leader—some guy who calls himself the Prophet—that his men shouldn't have touched the body, and that they needed to call the police, but he ignored me and ordered the men to take the dead man back to where they had found him, then report to him for a cleansing ritual."

"He refused to report the incident?" Graham's voice was calm, but his expression was one of outrage.

"He said they didn't have cell phones. Maybe they don't believe in them."

"Phones don't work in that area, anyway." Simon

Woolridge, the team's tech expert, spoke for the first time. "They don't work on most of the public land around here. No towers."

"That's why I didn't call you, either," Kayla said. "By the time I got a signal on my phone, I was almost here."

"Did anyone say anything about who the dead man might be?" Graham asked. "Did you recognize him?"

"No. Everyone looked as horrified as I did."

"Did the men do as the Prophet asked and take the body away?" Dylan asked.

"I don't know. I left before they did anything. No one tried to stop me. I wanted to get away from there and I headed straight here."

"What time was this?" Graham asked.

"I don't know. But it's a long drive. So…maybe an hour ago?"

"More like an hour and a half," Carmen said. "Dead Horse Canyon is pretty remote."

"Lieutenant Holt, I want you and Simon to check this out," Captain Ellison said. "Ms. Larimer, you ride with Lieutenant Holt and show him exactly where you were."

"We know where Dead Horse Canyon is," Simon protested.

"The canyon is seven miles long," the captain said. "She can show you the location more quickly."

Silently, Kayla followed Dylan to his Cruiser. He

opened the passenger door for her and she slid in without looking at him. He caught the scent of her floral shampoo as she moved past him, and he noticed the three tiny silver hoops she wore in each ear. By the time he made it around to the driver's side, she was buckled in and staring out the windshield.

"You holding up okay?" he asked.

"I'm fine." Her clipped tone didn't invite sympathy or further conversation, so he started the Cruiser and followed Simon out of the parking lot. They followed the paved road through the national park for the first five miles, past a series of pull-offs that provided overlooks into the Black Canyon, a half-mile-deep gorge that was the reason for the park's existence. Every stop was crowded with RVs, vans and passenger cars full of tourists who had come to enjoy the wild beauty of the high desert of western Colorado.

"How long have you been a private detective?" he asked.

She was silent so long he thought she had decided not to talk to him, but when he glanced her way she said, "Two years."

"Do you have a law enforcement background?" A lot of PIs he knew started out with police or sheriff's departments before hanging their shingle to do investigations, but Kayla hardly looked old enough to have had many years on the force under her belt.

"No."

"How did you get into the work?"

She let out a sigh and half turned to face him. "Why do you care?"

"I'm making conversation. Why are you so hostile?"

She ducked her head and massaged the bridge of her nose. "Sorry. I think I've just had an overdose of arrogant, good-looking men today."

She thought he was good-looking? He filed the information away for future reference. "I'm not trying to be arrogant," he said. "Cops are trained to get the facts of a situation as quickly as possible. That can come across as brusque sometimes."

She nodded. "I get that. It's just been a tough day. A tough week, really." She glanced at him, her expression a little less guarded. "I thought I was applying for a secretarial position when I answered the ad for the job," she said. "My boss got sick and trained me to take over the business. When he died from cancer last year, he left the business to me."

"And you like it enough to keep at it."

Another sigh. "Yeah, I like it. Most of the time. I mean, it beats a job in a cube farm. I like it when I can help people, even if it's just finding a lost pet or helping a woman locate her deadbeat ex so that she can collect child support. But you see the ugly side of people a lot."

"What you saw today wasn't very pretty."

"No."

She fell silent again, and he was sure she was back at the camp, picturing that bloody body again. He wanted to pull her away from the image, to keep her focused on him. "Who are the handsome, arrogant men who rubbed you the wrong way?" he asked.

"Daniel Metwater, for one."

"The Prophet of this so-called Family?"

"Yeah. Have you met him?"

Dylan slowed for the turn onto a faintly marked dirt track that veered away from the canyon and the park. "No. What's he like?"

"He talks a good game of peace and love and spirituality, or at least, that's what he writes in his blog. But it all sounds like a con game to me, especially considering he preaches about the futility of cell phones and technology, yet he has a website he updates often when he's away from the camp. Maybe I'm too cynical, but I wanted to shake all those women who were making cow eyes at him and tell them he didn't really care about any of them. He's the kind of guy who looks out for himself and his image first."

"What makes you think that?"

He halfway expected her to slap him down again. Instead, she relaxed back into the seat. "My dad was a charming swindler like Metwater—good-looking, silver-tongued and scary intelligent. His game was as a traveling preacher. I spent most of my childhood moving from town to town while he conned people out of whatever they would give him." She ran a hand through her hair, pushing it back from her face. "I guess that experience has come in handy in my work. I can usually spot a grifter as soon as he opens his mouth. Daniel Metwater may be preaching peace, love and communing with nature, but I think he's hiding something."

"Do you think he killed the guy you saw?"

"I don't know. It depends on when the guy died, I think. Metwater was standing with me for a good while before his followers dragged the body into camp. He was wearing white linen trousers and there wasn't a speck of blood or dirt on him, so he didn't strike me as a man who had just come from a murder."

"So you think the man was murdered."

"I think he had been shot. Whether the wound was self-inflicted or not is up to you people to determine." She shuddered. "I'm going to spend my time trying to live down the sight of him. The only dead people I've seen before were peacefully in their coffins, carefully made up and dressed in their Sunday best."

"Violence leaves an ugly mark on everything."

"Yeah, well, I guess you could say reality does that, too."

She turned away, staring out the side window, as unreachable as if she had walked into another room and closed the door. Dylan focused on the landscape around him—the low growth of piñon and scrub oak, and formations of red and gray rock that rose up against an achingly blue sky. He had grown up surrounded by this scenery. The country here didn't look desolate and hostile to him, as it did to some, but free and unspoiled.

Simon's brake lights glowed and he stuck his arm out the open driver's-side window, gesturing toward a gravel wash to their left. He stopped and the passenger window slid down as Dylan pulled alongside him. "That's the south entrance to Dead Horse Canyon," Simon said. "Where do we go from here?"

"Turn in here," Kayla said. "There's a trailhead about a quarter mile farther on. I parked there, but apparently the campers have been driving right into the camp."

"I'll follow you," Simon said, and waited for Dylan to pull ahead of him.

As camping spots went, this one lacked water, much shade or access, Dylan thought, as the FJ Cruiser bumped over the washboard gravel road into the canyon. But it did offer concealment and a good defensive position. No one would be able to approach without the campers knowing about it.

As if to prove his point, a bearded man in camouflage pants and shirt stepped into the road and signaled for them to stop. Dylan braked and waited for the man to approach the driver's side of the Cruiser. "You can't drive back here," the man said, his eyes darting nervously to the Ranger Brigade emblem on the side of the Cruiser. The words *Law Enforcement* were clearly visible.

"We're here to talk to Daniel Metwater," Dylan said. "Officers Woolridge and Holt."

"I'm not supposed to let anyone drive into the camp," the man said. He was sweating now, jittery as an addict in need of a fix.

"What's your name?" Dylan asked.

"Kiram."

Dylan waited for more, but Kiram had pressed his lips tightly together. "Well, Kiram, we're here on official business and you don't have the authority to stop us. We don't want trouble, but you need to step out of the way."

Kiram ducked his head and peered into the car. "Hey, what are you doing back here?" he asked Kayla.

"I brought them to see your dead body," she said, giving Kiram a chilly stare.

Dylan let off the brake and the Cruiser eased forward. Kiram jumped back. The two vehicles proceeded at a crawl up the wash, around the knot of trees and into the side canyon the Family had chosen as their home in the wilderness.

Dylan shut off the engine, but remained in the car, assessing the situation. The motley cluster of campers, tents and vehicles shimmered like a mirage in the midday heat. A child's ball rolled a few feet, stirred by the wind, which made the only sound in the area. "The place looks deserted," Kayla said. "Do you think they left?"

"Not without all their stuff. Do you notice anything missing?"

She studied the scene for a moment, then shook her head. "Only the people."

"Stay in the vehicle." With one hand hovering near his weapon, Dylan eased open his door, ready to dive for cover if anyone fired on them. But the camp remained silent and still.

"Daniel Metwater!" he called. "We need to ask you a few questions."

No answer came but the echo of his own words. Simon joined Dylan beside his car. "What do you think?" Dylan asked.

"They could have all headed for the hills, or they could be lying low inside these tents and trailers," Simon said.

"Come out by the time I count to ten or we'll start taking this place apart," Dylan shouted. "One!"

At the count of five, the door to the largest RV, a thirty-foot bus with solar panels on the roof, eased open. A slim but muscular man, naked except for a pair of white loose trousers, moved onto the steps. "I wasn't aware we had company," he said. "We adhere to the custom of an afternoon siesta."

"Are you Daniel Metwater?" Dylan asked.

Sharp eyes scrutinized the three of them. "Yes," he said at last.

"Call your people out here," Simon said. "We have some questions about an incident that happened here this afternoon."

Metwater shifted his gaze past the two cops. Dylan turned to see Kayla standing beside the car. "You had no cause to bring these people here," Metwater said to her.

"We're here because we understand you found a dead body this morning," Dylan said. "Why didn't you report it to the police?"

"We don't have cell phones, and since nothing we could do or say could bring the man back to life, I made the decision to report the incident the next time I was in town." Metwater spoke as if he was talking about a minor mechanical problem, not a dead man.

"Where is the body?" Simon asked.

"I ordered the men who brought him here to take him back where they found him," Metwater said. "They never should have defiled our home with such violence."

"We'll need to talk to these men."

"They are undergoing a purification ritual at the moment."

"Bring them out here." Simon wasn't a big man, but he could put a lot of menace and command in his voice. "Now."

Metwater said something over his shoulder to someone inside the RV. A woman with long dark hair slipped past him and hurried away. "She'll bring the men to you," Metwater said, and turned as if to go back inside.

"Wait," Dylan said. "Who was the man?"

"I don't know. I'd never seen him before in my life. But I believe he's one of yours."

"What do you mean, one of ours?" Dylan asked.

Metwater's lips quirked up in a smirk. "I checked his pockets for identification. He's a cop."

Chapter Three

Kayla watched Dylan as Metwater dropped his bombshell. His was a face full of strong lines and planes, not classically handsome, but honest—the face of a man who didn't have any patience with lies or weakness. Anger quickly replaced the brief flash of confusion in his eyes as he absorbed this new wrinkle in the case. The dead man wasn't a stranger anymore—he was a fellow lawman. "Take me to him," he ordered.

"The men who found him will—" Metwater began.

"No. *You* take me." Dylan's fists clenched at his sides, and Kayla tensed, expecting him to punch the smirk off the Prophet's face. But he remained still, only one muscle in his jaw twitching.

Instead of answering, Metwater looked away, toward a flurry of movement to their right. Kiram and another burly man escorted two other men to them. "These are the two who found the body," Metwater said. "They can answer your questions."

Dylan pulled a small notebook and pen from his

shirt pocket and shifted his focus to the new arrivals. Kayla thought they looked young, scarcely out of their teens, with wispy beards and thin bodies. Dylan pointed to the taller of the two, who stared back from behind black-framed glasses. "What's your name?"

"Abelard," the young man whispered.

"Your real name," Dylan said.

Abelard blinked. "That is my real name. Abelard Phillips."

"His mom was a literature professor," the other young man said. "You know, Abelard and Heloise— supposed to be a classic love story or something."

Abelard nodded. "Most people call me Abe."

Dylan wrote down the name, then turned to the second man. "Who are you?"

He swallowed, his Adam's apple bobbing. "Zach. Zach Crenshaw."

"I want the two of you to show me this body you found this morning."

Their heads moved in unison, like bobblehead dolls. Metwater started to turn back to his trailer, but Simon took his arm. "You're coming, too."

Kayla trailed along after them, sure that if Dylan remembered she was here he would order her to wait at the camp. But curiosity won out over her squeamishness about seeing the body again—that, and a reluctance to spend any time alone with the rest of the "family."

Single file, the six of them followed a narrow path

out of camp, out of the canyon and into the open
scrubland beyond, following drag marks in the dirt
Kayla was sure had been made by the makeshift tra-
vois Abe and Zach had used to transport the body.
She estimated they had walked about a mile when
Abe halted and gestured toward a grouping of large
boulders. "He's behind those rocks over there," he
said. "We put him back just like the Prophet told
us to."

"And you're sure that's where you found him?"
Simon asked.

Zach nodded. "You can tell because of all the
blood."

"Show me," Dylan said.

The two young men led the way around the boulders. Kayla hung back, but she still had a view of the
dead man's feet, wearing new-looking hiking boots,
the soles barely scuffed. Had he bought them especially for his visit to the Black Canyon area?

Dylan and Simon stood back, surveying the scene,
the wind stirring the branches of the piñons nearby
the only sound. The sour-sweet stench of death stung
her nostrils, but she forced herself to remain still, to
wait for whatever came next. "Was he lying like this
when you found him?" Dylan asked. "On his back?"

"Yeah," Zach said.

"Why did you move him?" Simon asked. "Were
you trying to hide something? Did you realize you
were tampering with evidence?"

"We weren't trying to hide anything!" Abe protested. "We just came around the rocks and almost stepped on him. There was blood everywhere and it was awful. Like something out of a movie or something. Too horrible to be real."

"Once we realized it was a man, we couldn't just leave him there," Zach said. "There were already buzzards circling. And I thought I heard him groan, like maybe he was still alive. We thought if we got him back to camp, someone could go for help, or take him to the hospital or something."

"We couldn't just leave him," Abe echoed.

"All right." Dylan put a hand on Abe's arm. "Tell me exactly what happened. Start at the beginning. What were you doing out here?"

"We were hunting rabbits," Abe said. "We thought we saw one run over here so we headed this way to check it out."

"What were you hunting with?" Simon asked. "Where is your weapon now?"

The two young men exchanged glances, then Zach walked over to the grouping of piñons. He reached into the tangle of branches and pulled out a couple crude bows and a handful of homemade arrows. "The Prophet only allows us to buy meat for one meal a week, so we thought if we could catch some rabbits the women could make them into stew or something," he said.

"And maybe they'd be impressed that we were

providing for the Family," Abe added. He looked even more forlorn. "We weren't having any luck, though."

"Why were you hunting with bows and arrows?" Simon asked. "Why not guns?"

"The Prophet doesn't allow firearms," Zach said.

"We're a nonviolent people." Metwater spoke for the first time since they had left camp. "Guns only cause trouble."

"They certainly caused trouble for this man." Dylan looked at Metwater. "You said you checked his identification?"

"The wallet is inside his jacket," Metwater said. "Front left side."

Dylan knelt, out of Kayla's view. When he stood again, he held a slim brown wallet. He read from the ID. "Special Agent Frank Asher, FBI." He fixed Metwater with an icy glare. "What was the FBI doing snooping around your camp, Mr. Metwater? And what did he do that got him killed?"

As EXPECTED, THE Family's Prophet claimed to have no knowledge of Agent Frank Asher or what had happened to him. None of the three men had heard any gunshots or vehicles or seen anything unusual in the hour leading up to the discovery of the body. They were like the three bronze monkeys Dylan's dad had on a shelf in his home office—see no evil, hear no evil, speak no evil. Dylan and Simon would bring them all in for questioning, but he doubted the interviews would yield anything useful.

With no cell phone coverage in the area, Dylan was forced to leave Simon with the body and the Family members while he drove to an area with coverage.

"I'm coming with you," Kayla said, falling into step beside him as he strode back toward the camp.

He'd been so intent on his job that for a while he had forgotten about her. She was one more complication he didn't need right now. "Why didn't you stay in the car like I told you?" he asked.

"This place gives me the creeps. I'm not staying anywhere alone around these people." She rubbed her hands up and down her arms. "Do you think one of them killed that FBI agent?"

"I don't know what to think. I need the medical examiner's report on when he died, and what kind of weapon killed him." He glanced toward the motley collection of RVs and tents. "I'm not buying that all of these people are unarmed."

"The agent will have a vehicle around here someplace close," Kayla said. "Those boots he was wearing weren't worn enough for him to have walked very far, and I didn't see a pack anywhere near him."

Dylan stopped and considered her more closely. She had regained her color and no longer looked fragile and shaken. "I'll get someone to look for the car right away. Maybe something in there will tell us why he was out here. That was a good observation," he added. "Did you see anything else?"

"I think the two kids are telling the truth." She glanced back in the direction they had come. "When they said that about not wanting to leave him for the buzzards—I believed them."

"Maybe." He had learned not to trust anyone when it came to crime, but his instincts made him want to focus on Metwater more than the two kids. "Them moving the body makes our investigation tougher. They may have destroyed a lot of evidence."

"For a man who sees himself as a leader, Metwater is a cold fish," she said. "He seemed more annoyed by the inconvenience than anything else."

"He's going to be a lot more inconvenienced before this is over. I'm going to get a warrant to take this camp apart. If the murder weapon is here, we'll find it."

"If it was ever here, they had plenty of time to get rid of it before we got here," she said. "It could be stashed in a cave or buried in an old mine or broken into a million pieces on the rocks."

"Maybe," he conceded. "But we might find something else incriminating."

They walked through the camp, which was as empty and silent as a ghost town, but he sensed people watching him from the windows of trailers and open flaps of tents. "Who did you come here to see?"

he asked Kayla. "I know you said a client's daughter, but who?"

"I don't see how that relates to your case." The frost was back in her voice.

"You're the one who reported the body. You were the only non-Family member present when it was discovered. Some people might think that was an interesting coincidence."

She turned on him, cheeks flushed. "You don't think I killed that man!"

"My job is to rule out everyone. Do you own a gun?"

"I have a Smith & Wesson 40 back at my office. I have a permit for it."

"But you didn't have it with you today? Why not?"

"I don't like to carry a gun. I didn't think this was a particularly dangerous situation."

"Who did you come to see?" he asked again. "I can subpoena your files to find out. Save us both some hassle and just tell me."

She hesitated, a deep crease between her brows as she weighed her options. "I came to see Andi Matheson. She calls herself Asteria now. But she doesn't have anything to do with your case."

"You said her father hired you. Who is he?"

She glared at him.

"I'll bet I can find the answer in five minutes or less online."

She continued to glare at him, and the intensity

of her gaze sent a thrill of awareness through him. Oh, he liked her, all right. Maybe a little too much, considering her involvement in this case.

"Her father is Senator Peter Matheson," she said. "I imagine you've heard of him."

Dylan had heard of the senator, all right. Until recently, he had been in the news primarily for his campaign to disband the Ranger Brigade. He had claimed the task force of federal agents was intrusive, expensive and ineffective. He had succeeded in having the group defunded, only to wind up looking like a fool when the Rangers had brought down a major terrorist group that had been operating in the area. Congress had responded by expanding the group, and Matheson had mostly kept a low profile ever since.

And now the senator was mixed up with Metwater and his bunch of wanderers. Dylan scanned the silent camp. "How did you track her down here? You said her father didn't know where she was."

"I talked to her friends. Her best friend told me she and Andi had attended a presentation given by Daniel Metwater and Andi had been very attracted to him, and to the ideas he preached. I did some more digging and verified that she had indeed joined up with Metwater and his group."

Dylan nodded. Textbook solid detective work. "Let's have a word with Ms. Matheson. Maybe she knows something she's not telling about all this."

"I really don't think—" Kayla began.

But Dylan had already moved to the nearest camper, a battered aqua-and-silver trailer wedged beneath a clump of stunted evergreens. He pounded on the door, shaking the whole structure. "Police! Open up!" he called.

A woman with a deeply tanned face and bleached hair eased open the door and peered out at them. "I'm looking for Andi Matheson," Dylan said.

The woman shook her head. "I don't know anyone by that name," she said, and started to close the door.

"What about Asteria?" Kayla asked. "Where does she live?"

"Over there." The woman pointed to a large white tent next to the Prophet's trailer.

The tent was the kind used by hunting outfitters as a mess tent or gathering area, with a tall frame and roll-up canvas sides. One of the sides was open to let in the hot breeze. Dylan moved around to the opening and peered in. A blonde woman sat cross-legged on a rug on the floor, eyes closed, hands out-stretched.

"Ms. Matheson?" Dylan asked. "Asteria?"

She opened her eyes, which were a deep blue. "I was meditating," she said.

"Sorry to interrupt, but I have to ask you a few questions." He took a step toward her. "I'm Lieutenant Dylan Holt, with the Ranger Brigade task force.

I wanted to ask you about the body that was brought to your camp earlier today."

Andi looked away. "I didn't see anything. I didn't want to look. It was horrible."

Kayla moved up beside Dylan, her voice gentle. "We don't want to upset you, Andi," she said. "We just have a few questions and then we'll leave you alone."

"All right." She motioned toward the rug across from her. "You might as well sit down."

The room was furnished with a cot and several folding camp chairs, but Dylan lowered himself to the rug. The coolness of the earth seeped up through the rug's pile. Kayla sat beside him. "Tell me what you saw this morning," he said.

Andi shrugged. "I didn't see much. There was shouting, and Abe and Zach came in, dragging something on a tarp. I thought they had killed an animal at first—there was so much blood. Then I saw it was a man and I looked away. I ran back here and hid." She rubbed her hand across her stomach. "I didn't want to see any more."

"Do you know a man named Frank Asher?" he asked. "He works for the FBI."

"Frank?" She stared at him, eyes wide. "What about Frank?"

"Did you know him?" Dylan asked.

"No!" She shook her head, hands clutching her

skirt. "No," she repeated in a whisper, even as tears ran down her face.

"I think you did know him," Dylan said. "Frank Asher is the man who was killed—the body Zach and Abe found this morning."

Andi covered her mouth with her hand. "I told him not to come here," she said, the words muffled. "I told him not to come and now look what happened." She collapsed onto the rug and began to sob, the mournful wailing filling the tent and making Dylan's chest hurt.

Chapter Four

Kayla knelt beside Andi, alarmed by the speed at which the beautiful, defiant young woman had dissolved into this wailing heap of grief. "I'm so sorry," she said, rubbing Andi's back. "Please sit up and try to calm down." She looked back over her shoulder at Dylan, who looked as if he wanted to be anyplace but here at this moment. "Would you get her some water?" She pointed toward a large jug that sat on a stand at the back of the tent.

He retrieved the water and brought it to her. "What was your relationship to Frank Asher?" he asked. "When was the last time you were in contact with him?"

The questions brought a fresh wave of sobs. Kayla glared at him. Did he have to act like such a cop right now, firing official-sounding questions at this obviously distraught woman? "You're not helping," she said.

Frowning, he backed away.

"Drink this." Kayla put the cup of water into Andi's hands. "Take a deep breath. You've had a shock."

"What's going on in here? What are you doing to her?"

The outraged questions came from one of the women Kayla had seen with Andi earlier—a slight figure with a mane of brown curly hair and a slightly crooked nose. She rushed over and inserted herself between Andi and Kayla. "Asteria, honey, what have they done to you?"

"What's your name?" Dylan joined them again.

The brown-haired woman glared at him. "Who are you, and why are you upsetting my friend?"

"Lieutenant Holt." Dylan showed his badge. "I'm investigating the death of the man whose body was brought into the camp earlier today. What's your name?"

"Starfall."

Kayla thought Dylan was about to demand she tell him her real name, but he apparently thought better of it. "Were you here when Abe and Zach brought him in?" he asked.

Starfall wrinkled her nose. "They should have known better than to pull a stunt like that. It was awful."

"What do you mean, 'a stunt like that'?" Dylan asked.

"The man was dead. I mean, half his head was gone. We couldn't do anything for him. They should have left him where they found him and not involved us in whatever happened to him."

Andi began keening again, rocking back and forth. Starfall wrapped her arms around her friend. "You need to go," she said. "You've upset her enough."

"Do you know a man named Frank Asher?" Dylan asked.

"No. Now go. You have no right to harass us this way."

Kayla touched Dylan's arm. "Give her a chance to calm down a little," she said softly. "You can question her later."

He nodded and led the way out of the tent.

The camp was just as deserted as it had been before. "Looks like nobody wants to take a chance on running into a cop," Dylan observed.

"Or maybe they really are taking a siesta." She pulled the front of her shirt away from her chest, hoping for a cool breeze. "It's baking out here."

He glanced back at her. "You should wear a hat." He touched the brim of the fawn-colored Stetson that was part of his uniform.

They left the camp, back on the trail to the parking area. "What are you going to do next?" Kayla asked.

"There's so much that feels wrong here it's hard to know where to start." He gave her a hard look. "What's Andi Matheson's relationship to Frank Asher?"

"How should I know?"

"Her father hired you to find her. You must have

looked into her background, talked to her friends and people who knew her."

"I did, but none of them ever mentioned a Frank Asher." No one had mentioned any men in Andi's life, outside of her father and a few very casual acquaintances. None of the photos and articles Kayla had viewed online linked Andi with a man. At the time, Kayla had thought it was a little unusual that a woman as attractive and seemingly outgoing as Andi didn't have a boyfriend, or at least an ex-boyfriend.

"Maybe he wasn't a friend of hers then," Dylan said. "Maybe her father knew him. It's not unreasonable to think a senator would know an FBI agent. Maybe you weren't the only person the senator had tailing his daughter. Maybe he sent the Fed after her, too."

"Or maybe Asher is the father of Andi's baby."

Dylan stopped so abruptly she almost plowed into him. "She has a baby?"

"She's pregnant. Didn't you notice?" Kayla gestured toward her own stomach.

He flushed. "I thought maybe she was just a little too fond of cheeseburgers or beer or something." He patted his own flat belly.

She stared at him. "I can't believe you said that."

"What did you expect? I'm a cop and a rancher— two professions known for plain speaking." He started walking again, long strides covering ground quickly so that she had to trot to catch up with him.

"You're a rancher?" she asked.

"My family has a ranch near here. In Ouray County." He pulled out his keys and hit the button to unlock the FJ Cruiser.

That explained a lot—from the way he seemed so at home in this rugged landscape, to the swagger in his walk that was more cowboy than cop.

He climbed in and started the engine even before she had her door closed. "If Asher is the father of Andi's baby, it would explain why she was so torn up over the news of his death," he said as he put the vehicle in gear and guided it onto the washboard road. "But why would she have told him to stay away from the camp?"

"I thought she joined the Family to get away from her father and his lifestyle," Kayla said. "But maybe she was trying to get away from Asher. Maybe he was the one who wanted her to get rid of the baby. Or maybe he was abusive."

"Would she carry on like that over a man who had abused her?"

"I don't know. Love can make people do crazy things, I guess." After all, her own mother had followed Kayla's father across the United States and back, sticking with him even when he cheated on her and lied to her.

"Are you speaking from personal experience?"

The question jolted her. "Why would you even ask something like that?"

"I'm just curious." He kept his gaze focused on the road, but she sensed most of his attention was fixed on her. "Something in the way you said that made me think you don't have too high an opinion of love."

She hugged her arms across her chest. This was *not* a conversation she wanted to be having. "I'm no expert on the subject. Are you?"

"Far from it. I've managed to avoid falling in love—serious love—so far."

"You make it sound like an accomplishment."

"I don't know. Some people might consider it a failing. My job doesn't really leave a lot of room for close relationships."

"Yet you have time to help run your family's ranch."

"Family is important to me. Which is why I don't get why Andi Matheson wanted to leave hers to live out in the wilderness with a bunch of people she hardly knows."

"Not everyone has a family they care to be close to—and yes, I say that from personal experience."

"Right—your con-artist dad. What about your mom? Brothers and sisters?"

"My mom is dead. I didn't have any siblings."

"I'm sorry to hear that."

"I don't want your pity."

He glanced at her, surprising warmth in his brown eyes. "Sympathy and pity aren't the same things."

She turned away, conversation over. She didn't

like not being in control of a conversation. One of the advantages of being a private investigator was that she usually got to ask all the questions. Situations like this one always made her feel like a freak. She didn't do relationships. Not close ones. She couldn't relate to people like Dylan, with his warm family feelings and determination to figure her out.

He apparently got the message and stopped talking. She focused on breathing deeply and getting her emotions under control. They passed through a brown sea of sagebrush and rock, beneath an achingly blue sky, unbroken by a single cloud. She would never get used to how vast the emptiness was out here. The wilderness made her feel small, lost even when she knew where she was.

He stopped the Cruiser and shifted into Park. "Why are you stopping?" she asked.

"I've got a phone signal." He dragged his finger across the screen on his phone. "I'm going to call in to headquarters."

He gave whoever answered the particulars of the situation at the camp and asked them to send crime scene techs and a medical examiner, along with more Rangers to interview people at the camp. "Simon is waiting," Dylan said. "I'm going to see if I can locate Asher's vehicle."

He ended the call and pocketed the phone, then put the Cruiser in gear once more. Neither of them said anything for several minutes as they bumped over increasingly rugged terrain. Finally, Dylan spoke. "I apologize if my questions were out of line," he said. "It's another cop thing. I want to know everything about people I'm with. I didn't mean to upset you."

His words touched her, and made her feel a little vulnerable. In her experience, people rarely apologized. "I didn't mean to snap," she said. "I'm just—on edge. Seeing that body, and then Andi falling apart like that—I guess it hit me harder than I realized."

"You're a very empathetic person," he said. "You feel other people's pain. You absorb their emotions. It probably makes you a good investigator, but it's tough."

"I guess so." She didn't really think of herself that way. If anything, she would have said she was too cynical most of the time.

He braked and pointed ahead of them. "What's that, up there?"

She caught the glint of sunlight off metal. "Maybe it's a car."

Dylan shut off the engine. "We'll walk from here."

He led the way toward the white sedan, which was partially hidden behind a clump of scrub oak. A small sticker on the bumper identified it as a rental car. When they were approximately ten feet away, Dylan held out his arm. "Stay here while I check it out," he ordered.

She waited while he approached the car. He peered

in the front driver's-side window, which had been left open a few inches. Then he pulled a pair of latex gloves from his pocket and put them on. He opened the driver's-side door, which wasn't locked, and peered into the car. Then he withdrew his head and looked back toward Kayla. "You can come up here if you promise not to touch anything."

She joined him beside the car. He had leaned in and was looking through a handful of papers on the front passenger seat. "There's a couple of maps here and a Montrose visitor's guide," he said.

"The parking pass on the dash is from a motel in Montrose," she said. "That's probably where he was staying."

Dylan examined the pass, then pulled out his note-book and began making notes. "I don't see anything out of the ordinary, do you?" he asked.

The only other thing in the car was a half-empty water bottle in the cup holder between the seats. "It doesn't look like he planned to be out here long," she said. "There are no snacks or lunch, no pack or change of clothes."

"So he either figured on a quick trip or he headed out here on impulse, not taking the time to prepare." Dylan opened the glove box, which was empty ex-cept for registration papers and the vehicle service manual. He flipped down both visors. The passen-ger side revealed nothing, but next to the mirror on the driver's side was a photograph.

Or rather, half a photograph. A tear was evident on the left side of the picture, a color snapshot of a man in jeans and a button-down shirt. Daniel Metwater's smiling face stared out at them.

"Maybe Andi wasn't the person Agent Asher came here to see," Dylan said.

Chapter Five

Dylan retrieved an evidence envelope from his Cruiser and sealed the photograph of Metwater in it. He took a few pictures of the vehicle and wrote down the plate number and the GPS location. "Let's go," he told Kayla as he pocketed his notebook. "I'll take you back to your car. You'll need to give us a statement about what happened at the camp this morning, then you can go. I'll probably have more questions for you later." He wanted to dig deeper into what she knew about Andi Matheson and the Family. And he wanted to see her again. Her mix of cold distance and warm empathy intrigued him.

"Do you do this kind of thing often?" he asked.

"What kind of thing?"

"Finding missing persons. Tracking down wayward children."

"Andi wasn't a lot of trouble to find. She just didn't want to talk to her father. Senator Matheson thought I might be able to get through to her."

"Seems an uncomfortable position to be in— caught in the middle of a family quarrel."

He wondered if she looked at everyone so intently, as if trying to decipher the hidden meaning behind every word he said. He wanted to protest that he didn't have an ulterior motive in talking with her, but that wasn't exactly true. He was trying to figure out what made her tick. Maybe she was doing the same to him. "A lot of my work involves dealing with people in one kind of pain or another," she said. "Whether it's a divorce or estranged families, or investigating some kind of fraud. Isn't it the same for cops?"

"Yeah." Too much pain sometimes. "You learn pretty quickly to distance yourself."

"My father made his living by preying on people's emotions. He was an expert at making people afraid of something and then offering himself as the way out of their trouble—for a price. I think seeing him in action made me wary of letting others get too close." Her eyes met his, dark and searching.

"Is that a warning?" he asked.

"Take it however you like."

Neither of them said anything on the rest of the drive back to Ranger headquarters. Carmen met them at the door to the offices. "A crime scene team is on its way out to meet Simon," she said.

"I found the victim's car, parked not too far away." Dylan read off the plate number and location.

"I'll call it in," Carmen said. "Some of the team might still be in cell phone range."

"I'll call them," he said. "I'd like you to take Kayla's statement."

"All right." Carmen sent him a questioning look. He knew she wondered why he didn't take Kayla's statement himself. He wasn't ready to admit that the dynamic between him and the pretty private detective was too charged. He couldn't be as objective about her as he liked and that bothered him. He wasn't one to let a woman get under his skin. "I'll be in touch later," he told Kayla, and turned away.

KAYLA WATCHED DYLAN leave the room, annoyed that his dismissal of her bothered her so much. So much for the detachment she'd bragged about. This cowboy cop, with his probing questions and dogged pursuit of information, drew her in.

"There's an empty office back here we can use." Officer Redhorse led the way to a room crowded with two desks and a filing cabinet. She sat behind one desk and indicated that Kayla should sit across from her. "Have you been a private investigator long?" Carmen asked.

"A couple of years."

Carmen opened up a file on the computer, then set a recorder between them. "Why don't you tell me everything that happened, from the time you arrived at the Family's camp this morning," she said. "I'll ask questions if I need you to clarify anything for me."

Kayla nodded, and took a moment to organize her thoughts. Then she told her story, about approaching the camp, and the two men bringing in the body. Carmen asked a couple questions, then typed for a few minutes more. "I'll print this out and you can read it over and sign it," she said, and swiveled away from the computer. "What happened when you and Dylan went back out there?" she asked.

"Are you going to compare my story to his?" Kayla asked.

"I'm curious to get your take on things," she replied. "Women sometimes notice things men don't— emotions and details men don't always pick up on."

"I don't think Lieutenant Holt misses much," Kayla said.

"He's new here, so I don't know him well," Carmen said. "Though he must be good at his job or he wouldn't have been assigned to the task force."

"He told me his family has a ranch in the area."

"The Holt Cattle Company. It's a big spread south of town. Knowing the country and the people here could be an advantage in this kind of work. Are you from the area?"

Kayla nodded. "But not knowing everyone can be an advantage, too. You don't come into a job with any preconceived notions."

"So what's your impression of the lieutenant?"

Kayla stiffened. "Why are you asking me?"

"I thought I sensed a few sparks between the two of you—though maybe not the good kind. Did you two have some kind of disagreement?"

"No disagreement." The two of them had worked well together, even though he sometimes made her feel prickly and on edge—too aware of him as a man who read her a little too well for comfort.

Carmen stood. "I'll get your statement off the printer and you can read through it."

When she was alone in the room, Kayla sagged back against the chair. Only a little longer and she would be free to leave. She wanted to do some investigating of her own, to try to make sense of what had happened this afternoon.

"I WANT A warrant to search Asher's hotel room," Dylan told Captain Ellison. The two stood outside Graham's office, Dylan having filled him in on his findings at the camp. "That might give us a clue what he was doing out there."

Graham nodded. "What about this PI? Kayla Larimer? Does she have any connection to Asher?"

"I don't think so. I'll talk to Senator Matheson to verify her story, but I think she was doing what she said—delivering a message to the senator's daughter."

"Did you learn anything else from her while you were at the camp?" Graham asked.

He had learned a lot—mainly that Kayla Larimer wasn't the type of woman to get close to anyone very easily. "She's good at her job, I think," he said. "Observant. She pointed out right away that Asher had to have a car nearby, after noting that his boots were new, the soles barely scuffed. And she was good with the women at the camp. She thinks Andi Matheson was so distraught over Asher's death because they had a close relationship. He may even be the father of her baby."

"What do you think?" Graham asked.

"Maybe. But Andi might have been distraught because of what she'd seen when the body was dragged into camp. It was enough to upset anyone. And the picture I found in Asher's car was of Metwater, not Andi. Asher may have had something on the Prophet that got him into trouble."

"I've got a call in to the Bureau, asking if Asher was here working on a case," Graham said. "Meanwhile, maybe his hotel room will turn up something."

"Are you going to Agent Asher's hotel?" Kayla asked.

Dylan turned to find the private detective, followed by Carmen, emerging from an office at the back of the building. "I want to go with you to the hotel," Kayla said, joining him and the captain.

"This is a police matter," he said. "You don't have any business being there. You know that."

She opened her mouth as if to argue, but apparently changed her mind. "Fine. Obviously, you don't have a need for me any longer, so I'll say goodbye." She nodded to Carmen and the captain, but didn't look at Dylan.

The snub irritated him. "I might have more questions for you later," he said.

"Maybe I'll have answers." She left, closing the door a little more forcefully than necessary behind her.

"I don't think she likes you too much," Graham observed.

"Oh, I don't know about that," Carmen said.

"What's that supposed to mean?" Dylan snapped.

"If she really didn't care what you thought, she wouldn't react so strongly." Carmen shrugged.

Dylan turned to Graham, and was surprised to find the captain grinning at him. "What are you smiling about?"

"My wife acted as if she hated my guts the first time we met," he said. "Carmen may be on to something."

Dylan turned away. "I'm going to file for that warrant." And he would do his best to forget all about Kayla Larimer. The last thing he needed was a woman who wanted to play mind games.

KAYLA SCARCELY NOTICED her surroundings as she drove toward town after leaving Ranger headquarters. She had to find a way to see what was in Frank Asher's hotel room. Lieutenant Holt might believe she had no right to get involved in this case, but he had made her a part of it when he took her back to the camp. She couldn't drop the matter now, with so many unanswered questions. And it wasn't such a stretch to see the FBI agent's death as linked to the assignment she had taken on for Senator Matheson. Agent Asher's murder had definitely upset Andi, and Kayla needed to know why.

Even if she had never met Dylan Holt and overheard him discussing searching Asher's hotel room, visiting the hotel would have been the next logical step in her own investigation. She didn't have the authority of a law enforcement agency behind her, but part of being a good private investigator was using other means to gain information. She might be able to charm a hotel clerk into letting her see the room, or to persuade a maid to open the door for her.

She wouldn't interfere with the Rangers' work. But she'd find a way to make Dylan share his information with her. She could even prove useful to him—another set of eyes and ears with a different perspective on the case.

She flipped on her blinker to turn onto the highway and headed toward the Mesa Inn—the name on the parking pass in Asher's car. She found a parking place in a side lot that provided a good view of the hotel's front entrance and settled in to wait.

She didn't have to wait long. Less than half an hour passed before two Ranger Cruisers parked under the hotel's front portico. Dylan and Carmen climbed out of the first one, while two officers she didn't recognize exited the second vehicle. As soon as the four were inside, Kayla left her car and headed toward the hotel's side entrance.

As she had hoped, it opened into a hallway that wound around past the hotel's restaurant and gift shop, to the front lobby. A large rack of brochures shielded Kayla from the Rangers' view, but allowed her to spy on them as they spoke first to the front desk clerk, then to a woman in a suit who was probably the manager. She wasn't close enough to hear their conversation, but after a few minutes the manager handed over a key card and the four officers headed for the elevator.

Kayla put aside the brochure for a Jeep rental company she had been pretending to study and walked quickly to the elevator. She hit the call button. The car the agents had entered stopped on the fifth floor before descending again. Smiling to herself, Kayla found the entrance for the stairs and began to climb.

On the fifth floor, she eased open the door to the hallway a scant inch and listened. The rumble of men's voices reached her. She was sure one of them was Dylan's. Risking a glance, she opened the door wider, in time to see the four officers enter a room in the middle of the hall. Kayla stepped into the hall and checked the number on the room—535.

Now what? She couldn't just barge in—that was

a good way to get arrested. And she didn't want to interfere, but she wanted information.

A loud squeak made her flinch. She turned to see a maid pushing a cleaning cart down the hall. Kayla moved toward her. "Excuse me," she said. "I wonder if you could answer a few questions about the man who was renting room 535." She opened her wallet and the maid, who looked like a student from the nearby university, stared at the badge. It clearly identified Kayla as a private investigator, not a cop, but most people didn't bother to read the fine print.

"Why do you want to know about him?" the woman—her name tag identified her as Mindy—asked.

"He's part of a case I'm working on."

Mindy bit her lower lip. "I don't know if I'm allowed to talk to anyone about the guests."

"Any information you provide could be very helpful," Kayla said.

Mindy pulled a cell phone from the pocket of her uniform top. "I'd better check with my manager."

Kayla held her breath while Mindy put through the call. If the worst happened, she could make a break for the stairs, or bluff her way out of this. But when Mindy explained there was a woman cop who wanted to question her, the manager apparently told her to cooperate. Good thing Carmen was along on this job. The manager probably assumed Kayla was her. "What do you want to know?" Mindy asked, as she slipped the phone back into her pocket.

"Did you see the man who rented that room? Did you speak to him?"

"I saw him," Mindy said. "But we didn't talk or anything. I saw him when he left the room yesterday morning."

"How did he act when you saw him? What kind of a mood was he in?"

Mindy shrugged. "I only saw him for a few seconds. He just looked, you know, ordinary."

"Did you clean his room? Did you notice anything unusual about it?"

"No. I mean, it's not like I spend that much time in the rooms. I clean them and get out."

"So nothing about this guy stood out for you?"

Mindy rearranged the bottles of cleaning solution in the tray at the top of her cart. "Not really." She avoided looking at Kayla.

"What is it, Mindy? Anything you remember— even a little detail—might be helpful."

"It's nothing, really."

"Even if you don't think it's important, it could be."

"Promise you won't tell my boss? We're not supposed to spy on the clients, you know? I could get in a lot of trouble."

"I won't tell." Kayla would probably never even see the manager.

"I was cleaning the room next door yesterday."

She nodded to room 533. "And I overheard the guy in 535. I think he must have been on the telephone, because I only heard one side of the conversation."

"What was he talking about?" Kayla asked.

"I don't know. I couldn't make out the words or anything, but he sounded angry or upset. He was shouting, you know?"

Kayla nodded. "That's very helpful. Could you make out any words at all?"

"Well…I think he said something like 'You can't do this' or something like that."

"Anything else?"

"No. I felt bad about eavesdropping that way, so I turned on the vacuum and went back to work. Did he do something bad?"

"No, he didn't. Thank you. You've been very helpful."

Mindy resumed pushing her cart down the hallway. She had scarcely passed 535 when the door opened and Dylan stepped out. He spotted Kayla before she could duck out of the way. "What are you doing here?" he demanded.

Chapter Six

"Hello, Lieutenant." Kayla gave him a cool look. "I've been waiting for you."

He moved closer, crowding her a little, frankly trying to intimidate her. "What are you doing here?" he asked again, his voice low, but not hiding his anger.

"I'm conducting my own investigation," she said. "I've been talking to the maid and she gave me some interesting information about Agent Asher." Her eyes met his and his heart beat a little faster. She wasn't the prettiest woman he had ever met, but those eyes, so changeable and expressive…

He mentally shook himself. "You shouldn't be here. You're not part of the investigation." Not entirely true. But she wasn't an official part of his team.

"I am. I won't get in the way, but I need to see."

"To see what?"

"I need to see what kind of man he was. To figure out his relationship with Andi. Her father is going to want to know."

"I could charge you with interfering with our investigation."

"I'm not interfering. Senator Matheson hired me because he's concerned about his daughter's safety. It's possible Agent Asher was a threat to that safety, or that he knew of a threat." She raised her chin, defiant.

He took a step closer and lowered his voice. "You're not going to back down, are you?"

"Did you really think I would?"

No. Part of him—the part that wasn't a cop—would have been disappointed if she had. "I could put you in cuffs and escort you out of here."

"Oh, you'd like that, wouldn't you?" Her voice took on a throaty purr, sending a jolt of pure lust through him.

He struggled to regain control of the situation, and of himself. "I can't let you into Asher's room," he said.

"I know, but you can tell me what you find in there."

"No, I can't."

"Tell me if you find anything to do with Andi and I'll tell you what I learned from the maid."

"I can interview the maid myself."

"Come by my place when you're done here and we can talk."

He shook his head. "No."

"I'll feed you dinner."

"I'm not going to tell you anything."

"I'll still feed you."

Spending an evening alone with Kayla wouldn't be the smartest move he had ever made. She was a witness in his case and a big distraction he didn't need.

She was also the most intriguing woman he had met in a long while. "All right."

The door to Asher's room opened again and Ethan and Carmen emerged, carrying stacks of evidence bags. Ethan glanced at Kayla. "What's she doing here?"

Dylan ignored the question. "Did you get everything?" he asked.

"I think we're done here," Ethan said.

"I'll meet you downstairs," Dylan said. "I want to take one more look."

Ethan looked at Kayla again, then shrugged and headed toward the elevator.

Kayla followed Dylan to the door of the room. "You can't come in," he said.

"I know."

She was smiling when he closed the door in her face. He tried to figure out what the smile meant. Did she think she had got the better of him? They were supposed to be on the same side here—both interested in solving a murder and upholding the law. But he didn't trust her. If her father was a con artist, maybe she had learned a few tricks from him.

KAYLA LEANED AGAINST the wall, arms crossed over her chest. Why had she invited Dylan to dinner at her place? It wasn't as if her cooking was going to work as a bribe. Maybe he thought she intended to seduce information out of him. The idea sent heat curling through her belly. She had walked a little too close to the edge with that remark about the handcuffs, but she hadn't been able to resist. Seeing the cowboy cop angry had been intimidating, but also a big turn-on. There was something about him that got to her, and she wasn't sure if she liked it or not.

Which was probably why she had issued her invitation. She needed to figure out where things were going with them and what it meant. The fact that he had agreed to come by her place probably meant he was curious, too.

The elevator doors opened and Kayla straightened. Two men dressed in jeans and denim work shirts, one carrying a tool bag, emerged. They slowed when they spotted her, and exchanged a look she couldn't read, but the younger one, with brown eyes and olive skin, nodded at her as they passed. They walked to the end of the hall and passed through the door marked Stairs.

Kayla went back to watching the door to Asher's room. What was taking Dylan so long? The other cop had said they were finished, but Dylan must have found something else. Something to do with Andi?

She couldn't shake the idea that Asher and the young woman were connected somehow.

She pulled out her phone. If someone came along, she'd look like she was waiting for a friend, or had stopped to make a call. She pulled up an internet browser and typed in Asher's and Andi's names, curious to see what might pop up. She watched the spinning icon as the site loaded, then let out a screech as the phone was wrenched from her fingers.

A hand clamped over her mouth, while strong arms crushed her in a painful grip. She kicked out at her captor, but a second man moved in front of her and cuffed her on the side of the head. She stared at the workman who had passed her earlier—the one with the olive skin and brown eyes.

He glared at her, then grabbed hold of her feet and held them tightly, preventing her from kicking. Together, the two men dragged her down the hall toward the stairwell.

DYLAN STOOD BY the window in the hotel room and surveyed the stripped bed and open drawers. The team had taken the clothes from the closet and a laptop computer from the safe, as well as the sheets and personal items to analyze for any evidence. If Asher had entertained anyone in the room before going to the Family's camp, they would find evidence of that. Dylan hoped the files would reveal the agent's purpose for being in Colorado.

Kayla thought the FBI agent was here because of Andi Matheson, but Dylan saw Daniel Metwater as the key to this case. Asher had Metwater's picture in his car, and the so-called Prophet had been entirely too cool about the sudden appearance of the dead man in his camp.

Dylan moved toward the door. He couldn't waste any more time pondering this. He had to get back to headquarters and start sorting through evidence. He expected to find Kayla waiting for him in the hallway. She had acted as if she intended to stay around, but maybe he had misread her. They had agreed to meet tonight, and he could get her address from the statement she had given Carmen. Still, it bothered him that she hadn't said goodbye.

He started toward the elevator, but a flash of light near the floor caught his eye. He stopped and scooped up a phone. The screen showed a browser open to a search for Frank Asher and Andi Matheson. An icicle of fear stabbed Dylan. This was Kayla's phone. He was sure he had seen her with it earlier.

He glanced up and down the hallway, which was empty and silent. Kayla wouldn't have carelessly dropped her phone. And she wouldn't have left without having a last word with him. Something had happened to force her to leave in a rush—without her phone.

He tucked the device into his pocket and called the front desk from his own cell phone. "This is

Lieutenant Holt," he said. "Did a young woman with shoulder-length brown hair, about five-six, dressed in jeans and a button-down shirt, come through the lobby within the last five minutes?"

"No, sir," the clerk said. "No one has been in the lobby since your officers came through here."

"Thanks." He hung up the phone and returned to the hall. If Kayla hadn't passed through the lobby, she must have taken the stairs. He spotted the exit sign at the end of the hallway and sprinted toward it.

When he pushed open the door he caught the faint floral scent that lingered in the air—Kayla. Adrenaline pumping, he pounded down the steps. Below, he heard the sound of a door opening and closing.

He sped up, propelling himself down the stairs, bracing both hands on the railing and vaulting toward the ground floor. If he was wrong, he was going to look pretty foolish, barreling after her like this, but after a decade as a cop, he didn't think he was jumping to the wrong conclusion. Kayla was in trouble, and he couldn't afford to waste a minute. The ground-floor exit opened onto a concrete pad that faced a parking lot. A row of Dumpsters sat at the edge of the lot.

He spotted his quarry right away—two men dressed in denim pants and shirts, carrying Kayla between them. He started toward them just as one of them—the one carrying Kayla's feet—raised a gun and fired. The bullet pinged off metal and Dylan dived for cover behind the nearest Dumpster, the smell of old garbage washing over him in a foul blanket.

He drew his weapon and peered out from between two garbage receptacles. Kayla's kidnappers had positioned her in front of them now, using her as a shield. He couldn't risk a shot. He drew out his phone and dialed 911. "Two men have kidnapped a woman from the hotel by the airport," he said. "There's a state patrol officer there but he needs help." Then he hung up and immediately hit the button for his office. "I'm at the Mesa Inn in Montrose. Two men have kidnapped Kayla Larimer. Send everybody you can spare."

Only half a dozen cars were parked in this back lot. The kidnappers angled toward a dun-colored van, the kind that might have been used by a plumber. A few more yards and they would have Kayla in that van. He couldn't let them get away.

Ignoring the questions from the admin on the other end of the line, he stuffed the phone in his pocket and took aim at the van. The shot was painfully loud, echoing off the metal Dumpsters, but satisfaction surged through him as he watched the windshield of the vehicle explode into a million shards of glass.

The two men with Kayla froze. They shouted curses, though whether at Dylan or at each other, he didn't care. Kayla took advantage of their inattention to kick and flail. The larger of the two, who had hold of her shoulders, punched her savagely in the face. Dylan forced himself to look away, and fired another shot at the van, aiming for the front grille, hoping to hit the engine and disable the vehicle.

His ears were still ringing from the gunfire when the wail of a fast-approaching siren reached him. This brought a renewed wave of curses from the two men. The one holding Kayla's feet had dropped her and was firing at Dylan from behind a parked car, while the first man struggled to hold on to the woman.

Dylan squeezed off a barrage of shots that sent the shooter diving behind the car's bumper. Seeing his chance, he rushed forward and took cover behind another vehicle. He had the shooter in his sights now, and took careful aim.

The shooter's scream when he was hit sent his partner into a panic. The man shoved Kayla away from him, sending her sprawling on the pavement. Then he dived into the van. As a trio of police cars sped into the lot, he took off, tires screeching, heading in the opposite direction.

One of the black-and-whites took off after the van, while the other two skidded to a halt near Kayla and the downed man. Dylan pulled out his badge and stood, holding his gun at his side and his badge up. "I'm Lieutenant Dylan Holt with Colorado State Patrol," he called.

"What happened, Lieutenant Holt?" A trim, graying man who identified himself as Sergeant Connor moved toward Dylan while a second officer helped Kayla to sit. Two other officers knelt beside the shooter, who lay still on the pavement.

Dylan ignored his questioner and knelt beside Kayla. "Are you okay?" he asked.

She was bleeding from her lip, and a purpling bruise was swelling on the side of her face, but she nodded. "I'm okay." She touched a finger to the corner of her mouth and winced. "Or I will be."

"What happened?" Sergeant Connor asked again.

"I was waiting for Dylan—Lieutenant Holt—in the hotel hallway and those two men grabbed me from behind and dragged me down the stairs and out here." Kayla looked at Dylan intently. "Who were they?" she asked. "What did they want with me?"

He shook his head. "I have no idea."

Her gaze shifted to the man on the pavement. "Is he…?"

"He's dead," Sergeant Connor said, and took a step to one side to block Kayla's view of the body.

A Ranger Brigade Cruiser joined the other vehicles in the lot. Graham Ellison climbed out as Ethan Reynolds came running from the lobby. They silently assessed the situation, then strode over to join the others. "Graham Ellison. I'm the captain of the public lands task force." He offered his hand to Sergeant Connor.

"I've heard about you guys. The Ranger Brigade." Connor shook his hand. "We've got an ambulance on the way for the young lady."

"I don't need an ambulance." Kayla struggled to her feet. Dylan reached out to steady her as she swayed. "I'm just a little banged up," she protested, but didn't push him away. "I'll be fine."

"When you're able, we'll need you to come in and make a statement," Connor said.

"I'll tell you what little I know," she said. "But it all happened so fast I can't provide a lot of details."

"Did you recognize either of the men who grabbed you?" Dylan asked.

"No."

Connor's radio crackled and he turned away from them to answer it. But the rest of them clearly heard the message. "We have the suspect in custody," a man's voice said.

"We'll want to question him as soon as possible," Graham said. "He may be connected with a murder we're investigating."

Connor studied Dylan. "Tell me about this investigation," he said. "How does a crime on public lands connect to an attempted kidnapping in Montrose city limits?"

"There may be no connection," Dylan said. "But why would someone try to kidnap Kayla outside a room where the murder victim was staying?"

"Who was the murder victim?" Connor asked.

"A federal agent," Graham said. "Frank Asher. Did you know him?"

Connor shook his head. "Never heard of him. What was he doing in Montrose?"

"That's what we're trying to find out," Graham said. He turned to Kayla. "Let the EMTs check you out, then we'll get someone to take you home."

"I have my car here," she said. "I can drive myself."

"Someone can drop it by your place later," Graham said. "Until we know more about these men and why they grabbed you, we're going to keep a close eye on you."

She bristled. That was really the only way to describe it. She drew herself up straight and her hair all but stood on end. "I can look after myself."

"Nevertheless, we'll be checking in regularly," Graham said. "And if you spot anything out of the ordinary, call us."

"Or call *us*," Connor said.

The ambulance turned into the lot and stopped alongside them. Dylan left Kayla in the care of the EMTs and joined Graham and Ethan as they walked toward the hotel. "What was she doing here?" Graham asked.

"She followed me," Dylan said. "She thinks Asher is connected with Andi Matheson and she wanted to find out how."

"What did you tell her?" Graham asked.

"I told her she had no business being here and if she didn't leave I could have her arrested for interfering in our investigation."

"I take it she didn't leave," Ethan said.

"I left her in the hallway while I went back into the room." No way was he going to reveal he had agreed to have dinner with her. "When I came out, she was gone, but I found her phone where she had dropped it on the floor. I checked the stairs and saw those two dragging her away."

"How did they know you and Kayla were here at the hotel?" Graham asked.

"They could have followed us. Or maybe the desk clerk tipped them off."

"Or maybe it was bad timing," Ethan said. "They showed up to get something from Asher's room, saw Kayla waiting there and decided they had to get rid of her."

"It's a big risk to take," Dylan said.

"Maybe what they were after was that important," Graham said.

"We got everything from the room, so if there was something there, we'll find it," Dylan said.

"He wasn't on a case," Graham said. "His supervisors said he took two weeks' vacation, starting three days ago. They swear whatever he was doing down here was his personal business."

"Personal business that got him killed," Ethan said.

And almost got Kayla killed, Dylan thought. The idea chilled him.

"Agent Ellison!"

The trio turned to see Sergeant Connor hurrying toward them. "Something just came in I thought you'd want to know about," he said when he reached them. "We ran the plates on the vehicle the shooter was driving and it's registered to Senator Pete Matheson."

"Was it stolen?" Dylan asked.

"That's what we wondered," Connor said. "But when we ran a search for stolen vehicle reports, what we came up with instead was a missing person's report."

"Who's missing?" Graham asked.

"Senator Matheson. No one has seen or heard from him since Friday."

Chapter Seven

Kayla persuaded the Montrose police deputy who drove her home that she didn't want or need a bodyguard. She suggested—and the officer's supervisor agreed—that an occasional drive-by to verify all was peaceful in her neighborhood would be sufficient. She would lock herself in the house and keep both her gun and her phone close at hand.

When she was alone at last, she tried to do as the EMTs had recommended and rest, but every time she closed her eyes her mind replayed the morning's events, from the appearance of Agent Asher's body to Andi's anguished tears to those moments of terror when her kidnappers had held her and bullets whined past.

And Dylan—he disturbed her rest, as well. The man intrigued and aggravated her in equal parts. She told herself she wanted to know what he could tell her only so that she could help Andi and the senator, but deep down she knew she wanted to see Dylan again because she wanted the thrill she felt in his presence—a physical craving coupled with the sense that here was a man who might be worth opening up to.

Unable to sleep, she gave up and went to her computer and once more typed Andi's and Agent Asher's names into the search engine. She found plenty of articles about Andi, mostly mentions of her attendance at various society parties or fund-raisers, with and without her father. But the only mention she found of Asher was a talk he once gave to a neighborhood watch group in Denver. The Fed definitely kept a low profile.

The chime of her doorbell interrupted her thoughts. She started to the door, but froze as she caught a glimpse of herself in the mirror over the small table in the foyer. An ugly purple bruise spread across her left cheek and a black half-moon showed beneath her left eye. She put a hand to the bruising and winced. Apparently, she looked even worse than she felt.

The doorbell rang again. Sighing, she checked the peephole and spotted Dylan Holt rocking back and forth on his heels, staring back at her. She pulled away from the peephole. She didn't really want to see Dylan right now. Not looking like this. Not with her feelings so confused. What did you say to a man who had saved your life? She really wasn't good at this sort of thing. Not that it had ever come up before, but still...

The bell chimed again.

She undid the locks and pulled open the door. "If you came to check up on me, I'm fine," she said.

"I came for dinner." He pushed past her, a shopping bag in one hand.

She'd forgotten all about their dinner date, which felt as if it had been made in an alternate reality, before she'd been manhandled, dragged across a parking lot and shot at—or, at least, shot around. "I'll have to take a rain check," she said. "I don't exactly feel like cooking."

"You don't have to cook." He set the shopping bag on her dining table and began taking out cardboard to-go containers. "I hope you like Chinese."

The aroma of sesame chicken made her mouth water, and she realized she was hungry. Starving. She hurried to the cabinet and pulled out plates. Neither of them said anything else until they were seated across from each other at her small kitchen table with full plates. After a few bites of chicken and rice she paused and grinned at him. "Thanks," she said. "You may have just saved my life. Again."

His expression sobered. "I didn't come here just to feed you."

She put down her fork. "Did you find out anything about the men who attacked me?"

"The truck they were driving was registered to Senator Matheson."

"You mean it was stolen?"

"We don't know. When was the last time you spoke to Senator Matheson?" he asked.

"Friday afternoon. I told him I planned to visit the Family's camp and hoped to speak with Andi."

"How did he take the news?"

"He was pleased. He wanted me to try to persuade her to leave with me and return to his home. I told him all I could do was give her the message, but he seemed optimistic. He told me to call him as soon as I returned from talking with her, to let him know how she's doing."

"Did you call him?"

"Not yet. So much has been going on I haven't had time."

"Would you mind calling him now?"

"Why? What's going on?"

"Call him and then I'll tell you." Dylan softened his expression. "Please."

"All right." She reached into her pocket, then froze. "I can't find my phone."

He pulled the phone from his own pocket. "You must have dropped it when those two thugs grabbed you," he said.

"Thanks." That showed how rattled she had been—she hadn't even realized her phone was missing. She scrolled through her contacts and found the number for Senator Matheson. The phone buzzed a couple times, then a message came on that informed her the mailbox of the person she was trying to reach was full.

"That's odd," she said after she had ended the call. "He's usually good about checking his messages. But his mailbox is full."

"Is that his office number or a private line?" Dylan asked.

"It's his private cell phone, I think. Dylan, what is going on?"

"The senator's administrative assistant reported him missing this morning. He left his office Friday afternoon and was scheduled to attend a Senate hearing on finance today. No has seen him since then. You may be the last person who spoke with him. I expect it will be on the news any minute now."

"I haven't had the TV on. And I was doing research online, so I didn't notice the headlines. So what's the connection between the guys who attacked me and Senator Matheson? Did they steal the truck and kidnap him? And then they came to Asher's hotel to look for something?"

"To look for what?"

"I don't know—something incriminating? Something that linked them to both Asher and the senator?"

"You're linked to Asher and the senator. The senator hired you to track down his daughter at the camp and while you were there, Asher's body was found."

"So you think, what—that they followed me to the hotel? Why?"

"Maybe they think you saw something you shouldn't have."

"I didn't see anything."

"Then why did they kidnap you? Did they say anything to you?"

"They didn't say a word."

He scowled and bit down hard on a fried wonton. "I can't know you're safe until I figure out why those men grabbed you," he said.

"You don't have to worry about me." His concern unsettled her. "Besides, they're in custody, aren't they? I mean, the one who lived is." She wasn't likely to forget the sight of the man sprawled on the pavement—the second body she had seen that day. "I don't have anything to worry about."

"He's in the hospital," Dylan said. "With a police guard posted at his door. We haven't had a chance to question him yet. What if the attack wasn't their idea? What if someone hired them? He could hire someone else." He looked around the room. "Do you have a security system?"

"No. I don't need a security system."

"Maybe you shouldn't stay here tonight. At least until we get to the bottom of this."

"Lieutenant, I'll be fine. I have good locks, and a weapon if I need to use it. And I can always dial 911. The police station is only a few blocks away."

"I still don't like it." He attacked another wonton. "I'd think you'd be afraid to stay here alone after what happened to you today."

"I was fine until you came along with all these dire predictions of peril. Honestly, you're blowing everything out of proportion."

"Am I? You could have died today. I don't like the idea of someone trying again."

"I don't like that idea, either, but it's not going to do anyone any good for me to run around wringing my hands and fretting about it. I think I'm as safe here in my own home as I would be anywhere else. And I still think the attack on me was random—I was in the wrong place at the wrong time. Those two wanted me out of the way so they could get into the hotel room. They were even dressed like workmen."

"What did you find out when you talked to the maid?" Dylan asked.

"Not much," she admitted. "She said she overheard Asher on the phone with someone. He was arguing, but she didn't know what the argument was about."

"Maybe Asher was arguing with his killer."

"Maybe." She spooned more fried rice onto her plate. "What did your search of Asher's room turn up?"

He hesitated.

"Just tell me if you found anything to link him to Andi," she said.

"We don't know yet. He has files on his computer, but they're all encrypted. We've got people working on it." He dipped an egg roll in plum sauce and took a bite.

"Check his phone, too."

He swallowed. "Thanks. I hadn't thought of that."

She fought the urge to stick her tongue out at him. But perhaps they hadn't descended into such juvenile sparring yet. "I'm going to keep digging," she said.

"What did you learn about Andi and Asher?"

"How did you know I was researching them?"

"I saw the web page on your phone browser. Did you learn anything?"

She shook her head. "Asher has definitely kept a low profile, but maybe that's usual for a federal agent. All the mentions I found about Andi had to do with her father, or some society do she attended. She's certainly living a very different kind of life now."

"I'm going back out to the camp tomorrow to talk to Andi," he said. "I need to tell her about her father and find out if she's heard anything, and I intend to ask her about Asher."

"Let me go with you."

"No."

"She'll talk to me. You just frighten her."

"You make me sound like some kind of bully."

"Let's just say you can be pretty intimidating when you want to be."

"Do I intimidate you?" His eyes met hers and she felt that jolt of attraction again. She wasn't afraid of him, only of where these wild feelings she had for him might take her.

She wet her suddenly dry lips. "I don't know, Lieutenant—do *I* intimidate *you*?"

"*Intimidate* isn't the word I'd use." He leaned across the table toward her and cupped his hand along the side of her injured cheek, not touching her, but close enough that she could feel the heat of him. "You're a puzzle I want to figure out," he said.

She wanted to lean into him, to press her lips to his and learn if he would respond with the same boldness with which he questioned a suspect or faced down danger. But once she crossed that barrier with him, there wouldn't be any going back. Neither of them was the type to back down from a challenge.

The loud strains of Fergie sounded from her phone, making her jump. Dylan sat back, arms crossed on his chest. She avoided his gaze, checking the phone's screen instead. Not a number she recognized, but it could always be a new client—someone wanting her to spy on a cheating spouse or track down a long-lost relative. "Larimer Investigations," she answered.

"Is this Kayla Larimer?" a woman's voice asked.

"Yes."

"I have a message for you from Andi Matheson."

Kayla sat up straighter. "What is it?"

"She needs to talk to you. Can you meet her at the parking area for the Dead Horse Canyon Trail tomorrow afternoon at one?"

"What is this about?" Kayla asked. "Who is this?"

"I'm just a friend. I promised to call and give you this message. Can you meet her?"

"Yes, of course. But—"

The line went dead before she could ask any more questions. Kayla looked up and met Dylan's eyes. "Andi wants to meet me in the morning," she said.

"I'll go with you," he said.

"She said she wanted to talk to me—not you."

"I'll go with you." His expression was grim. "I don't trust these people. I'm not going to let you go alone."

DYLAN PICKED UP Kayla from her house the next afternoon. He had been tempted to insist on staying with her overnight—on her couch, though he wouldn't have turned her down if she had invited him into her bed. He didn't trust whoever was responsible for the attack on her not to make another try. But in the end he had decided alienating her by pushing to get his way wasn't worth the trouble. He had made her show him her gun and her locks, and he was satisfied both were adequate. Then he had touched base with the Montrose PD and impressed upon them the need to make a few extra passes by her house during the night.

He showed up a half hour early the next afternoon, since he didn't entirely trust her not to slip off by herself. While he admired independence in a woman, she seemed to want to take it too far. He still got chills when he thought about how close she had come to dying yesterday.

She met him in her driveway, her purse slung over one shoulder, a steaming mug in her hand. "I could have driven myself," she said.

Did he know her or what? "Good afternoon to you, too." He opened the passenger door for her. "Look at it this way—you're saving gas and wear and tear on your car."

She slid into the seat and reached for the seat belt. "Just remember, Andi wants to talk to *me*."

"I have to give her the news about her father and try to find out if she's been in contact with him since he disappeared." The FBI had handed that job off to the Rangers.

"So the senator is still missing?" she asked.

"Yes. Apparently, there's no sign of a struggle at his home or office, and no one has seen or heard from him since he left work Thursday." Dylan put the Cruiser in gear and backed out of her driveway.

"What about the man who attacked me? You said the van he was driving belonged to Senator Matheson? Does he know anything?"

"The senator used the van as a campaign vehicle when he ran for reelection two years ago, and some of his staff workers have used it occasionally since then," Dylan said. "We still haven't been able to interview the suspect, but our research hasn't turned up a connection." He glanced at her. "So we're agreed that I'll talk to Andi?"

"Fine. But let me talk to her first. I don't want you scaring her off before I find out what she wants."

"I thought we established last night that I'm not that scary."

She flushed. Was she remembering that moment when he had almost kissed her? His fingertips tingled at the memory, remembering the heat of her against his skin, and the almost overwhelming need he had had to touch her.

"You don't frighten me," she said. "But Andi may be another story."

He pulled to the stop sign at the end of her street. "Fine. You take the lead, but then I get to ask my questions."

"I think we've already established that you're good at questions." The amused glint in her eyes took the sting out of her words.

"That's right," he said. "When I was a kid my dad threatened to gag me with my own bandanna when we were out working and I'd pester him with too many questions."

He turned onto the highway and she settled back into the seat and sipped from her mug. "Do you like ranching?" she asked after a moment.

"I like being out-of-doors. I like working with the animals. But it can be frustrating. There's so much you can't control, from weather to cattle prices. And sometimes it's just a lot of hard work. I had to go away for a while to appreciate it."

"Where did you go?"

"To Denver. I was in law enforcement there for ten years after college. But I missed all this." He indicated the sweep of land out the windshield. "And my dad had some health problems and needed more help. When the opening for this job came up, I was glad to take it."

She didn't say anything and he wondered what she was thinking. From what little she had said about her past, he gathered she had never had a place she felt rooted to—a real home. She had come to Montrose almost by chance and had no ties here other than her job.

"This work must be different from what you did in the city," she said. "This isn't exactly a high-crime area."

"More goes on here than you might think," he said. "But a lot of it goes on behind the scene—drugs, theft of artifacts, smuggling. And a lot of people see public lands as a good place to hide out."

"People like Daniel Metwater."

"Yeah. How much do you know about him?"

"Not a lot," she said. "He started calling himself

a prophet and recruiting followers a little over a year ago. I take it he comes from money."

"His father was an industrialist named Oscar Metwater. When he died, Daniel and his twin brother, David, inherited the family fortune. David was killed a few months later in what was likely a mob hit. He had a gambling habit and had embezzled money from the family firm and apparently borrowed from the wrong people."

"In one of his official bios Daniel says something about his brother—about how his death made him see the futility of the life he had been leading and made him seek a better way."

"I guess some people would see having a slew of followers turn over all their possessions to you and do your bidding as a better way of life," Dylan said. "And from what I saw, the majority of those followers are beautiful young women."

"While some religions teach the importance of caring for the poor and afflicted, I'm guessing Daniel Metwater isn't one of them," she said.

"What about your father?" he asked. "Was he like Metwater?"

"Oh, he could quote scripture about widows and orphans when he thought it would encourage people to put more in the collection plate," she said. "But the only person he was really interested in looking out for was himself. Metwater strikes me as the same."

She shifted toward Dylan. "Do you know why Agent Asher had Metwater's picture in his car?"

"We haven't come up with anything yet. The computer forensics may take a while. Or we might find out something from Andi."

She fell silent and Dylan didn't try to engage her further. Maybe he shouldn't have brought up her father. Clearly, it wasn't a pleasant topic for her.

After a dusty ride on a rugged dirt track, they reached the parking area for the trail, marked only by a bullet-riddled brown sign. The Ranger Cruiser was the only vehicle in sight. Dylan pulled into the lot and shut off the engine, and silence closed around them. He scanned the outcropping of rocks and clumps of scrubby piñons and sagebrush for any signs of life. "This would be a good place for an ambush," he said.

His plan was to wait in the Cruiser until someone approached, but before he could say so, Kayla opened her door and got out. Almost immediately, Andi emerged from behind a large boulder, her long hair blown sideways in a gust of hot wind. She wore the same prairie skirt and tank top she had had on yesterday, a blue cotton shawl around her shoulders.

She eyed Dylan warily as he climbed out of the vehicle and came to stand behind Kayla. "What is he doing here?" Andi asked. "I wanted you to come alone."

"The person who called me didn't say anything

about that," Kayla said. "I thought it would be a good idea for him to come along for protection. You can't blame me for being nervous, after what happened to Frank Asher."

At the mention of Asher, Andi's lips trembled, but she brought her emotions under control. "Can I trust him?" she asked.

"Trust me with what?" Dylan said, ignoring the annoyed look from Kayla.

"Can I trust you to keep my confidences?" Andi asked. She wrapped her hands in the ends of the shawl. "I don't want certain people knowing about what I'm going to tell you."

"What people?" Kayla asked.

Andi shook her head and began walking away from them, toward the road. Kayla and Dylan fell into step alongside her, gravel crunching under their feet. "Do you mean Daniel Metwater?" Kayla asked. "Is that why you wanted to meet us away from the camp—so the Prophet wouldn't know you were meeting me?"

"Everyone in the camp is busy preparing for the ceremony this evening," Andi said.

"What kind of ceremony?" Kayla asked.

"We have a new member joining the Family. That's why I couldn't call you myself yesterday. I had to stay and help with the preparations. The woman who called was one of the ones chosen to go into town to buy food for tonight's celebration."

She fell silent again, and Dylan fought the urge to fire more questions at her. Maybe Kayla was right and he needed to let her take the lead here, at least until Andi was more comfortable with him. She was calmer today, though an air of sadness clung to her. The skirt she wore was faded, with a tear in the hem at the back, and the pink polish on her toes was chipped. As the daughter of a prominent senator, she was probably used to designer fashions and spa treatments. Was she growing disillusioned with life in the wilderness with the so-called prophet?

"How are you doing?" Kayla asked when they had walked another hundred yards or so. "You were pretty upset when I saw you yesterday."

"It was the shock of learning about Frank's death." She swept a lock of hair out of her eyes and tucked it behind one ear.

"You knew him, then," Kayla said.

"Oh, yes." She drew in a deep breath. "We were lovers. He's the father of my baby."

So Kayla had been right, Dylan thought.

"Was he coming here to see you?" Kayla asked.

"I don't know." Andi pulled the shawl more tightly around her shoulders. "I told him not to come—that I had nothing to say to him. We ceased being close months ago, before I even learned I was pregnant."

"Why did you break up?" Kayla asked.

She looked away, lips pressed tightly together.

"You probably think the answer to that question

is none of our business," Dylan said. "But if there's the slightest chance that the reason the two of you split up could have anything to do with his death, we need to know."

She shook her head, still not looking at them. "I'm sure it doesn't have anything to do with his death."

"We're in a better position to determine that," Dylan said.

"Frank was my father's friend before he was mine, and in the end, he had the same mindset. He was of that world. Isn't that enough?"

"So Frank Asher and your father knew each other?" Dylan asked. He kept his eyes on Andi, though he was aware of Kayla's frown. She wasn't pleased he was asking so many questions, but that was his job.

"Frank worked for my father," Andi said. "That's how we met."

"I thought he was an FBI agent," Kayla said.

"He took a year's leave from the Bureau to work as my father's private security agent. But when my father found out we were lovers, he and Frank argued and Frank went back to work for the Bureau." Andi turned and began walking again.

"When was the last time you saw Frank?" Kayla asked.

"Last week. He must have found out I was here and he stopped me in town and said we had to talk. I was with some of the other women and I told him I had nothing to say to him. He said he would come to the camp to talk to me. I told him not to, but he didn't listen. Men don't, do they? Not when it's a woman talking."

She didn't look at Dylan when she said the words, but he felt their impact.

"Do you know anything about what happened to him?" Kayla asked, her voice gentle.

Andi shook her head. "I was so shocked when you told me it was him." She hugged her arms across her chest. "That's why I wanted to talk to you today. I knew you would wonder why I was so upset over his death. Even though I haven't loved him for a while, at one time he meant something to me, so I grieve. And it saddens me to think my child will never know its father."

Kayla put a hand on Andi's shoulder. "I'm sorry for your loss. I'm sure it was a great shock."

Andi straightened. "Of course, the Prophet will be the child's father, as he is father to all of us."

"Is that how you see him?" Dylan asked. "As a father? You and he are close to the same age."

Andi glanced back at him. "Well, perhaps not a father. But he is our leader. Our guide." She brought the shawl up to cover her head. "We should go back now. I've said what I needed to say."

She led the way ahead, then faltered, stumbling. Dylan reached out to steady her, then froze as a man stepped from the brush alongside the road. Sunlight glinted off the lenses of his mirrored sunglasses, and off the pistol in his hand.

"If you want to know more about me, Lieutenant, you ought to talk to me," Daniel Metwater said.

Chapter Eight

Kayla stood very still, more fascinated than fearful, as Daniel Metwater strode toward them. Though not a large man, he exuded power, a kind of magnetic vitality radiating from him. He moved with a swagger, a gleam in his eyes that told her he was confident of the admiration of all who observed him. As much as she loathed his attitude, she could admit to being compelled by him. She understood why so many young women fell under his charismatic spell. The promise of being the focus of such raw energy and sex appeal could be intoxicating.

When he was a few feet away, he tucked the gun into a holster on his right hip. "Are you all right, Asteria?" he asked.

She nodded, her gaze focused on the ground.

Metwater turned his attention to Kayla and Dylan. "If you want to talk to me or one of my followers, it isn't necessary to sneak around outside the camp," he said. "We have nothing to hide."

"What are you doing with that gun?" Dylan asked. "I thought you preached nonviolence."

"As the unfortunate events of yesterday prove, the wilderness is not as safe a place as it would seem," he said. "And before you ask, we've had hordes of officers swarming over the camp searching for weapons. They have already examined this particular gun and determined it isn't the same caliber as the one that killed Agent Asher. And they haven't found any other guns among my followers."

"Why do you need a gun if you don't allow your followers to be armed?" Dylan asked.

"It is my job to protect my people."

"Have you been threatened in any way?" Dylan asked. "Have there been other incidents you haven't reported to the police?"

"No." He took Andi's arm and pulled her toward him. "Come back to camp now," he said. "You must be tired. You need to rest."

Kayla's skin crawled as she watched any hint of the young woman's personality vanish in Metwater's shadow. "Andi, you don't have to go with him if you don't want," she said.

"No, it's fine," Andi said. "My place is with him. With the Family."

Metwater fixed his gaze on Kayla, an intense scrutiny that made her feel naked and exposed. "You fear us because you don't understand us," he said. "You don't understand the security and refuge I offer my followers. We are having a special ceremony this evening to welcome a new Family member. I'm inviting you both to attend. It will help you to understand us better."

"All right, we'll be there." Dylan took Kayla's arm and squeezed it, cutting off her protest. She had no desire to spend any more time than necessary with Metwater and his followers, but if Dylan thought attending the ceremony would help in the investigation, she was willing to play along.

"Come along, Asteria." Metwater prepared to lead Andi away.

"Ms. Matheson, when was the last time you spoke to your father?" Dylan asked.

Andi stumbled. Only Metwater's grasp on her arm kept her from falling. She looked over her shoulder at Dylan. "My father?"

"Yes. When was the last time you were in contact with him?"

"Months ago," she said. "We haven't spoken since I joined the Family."

"You haven't heard from him recently, in the past few days?"

"She told you she hasn't," Metwater said. "We're leaving now. We'll see you both this evening. Come at dusk and someone will be waiting to escort you to the ceremony."

"Andi, have you heard from your father in the past few days?" Dylan asked again.

She shook her head. "No."

"I'm sorry to have to tell you he's missing."

Andi's expression didn't change. "I don't know anything about that." Then she turned and, holding Metwater's hand, walked away.

Kayla frowned after her. Dylan nudged her. "Let's get out of here."

Neither of them spoke as they made their way back to Dylan's Cruiser, but once they were inside the vehicle, he turned to her. "Does it strike you as cold that Andi didn't react to news of her father's disappearance? She certainly cried buckets over Frank Asher."

Kayla nodded. "Something was off about her reaction—maybe because Metwater was there."

"But we're talking about her father. Her only living parent."

"I wouldn't necessarily have much of a reaction if you told me my father was missing," she said. Her father had been missing from her life—or at least, the fatherly part of him had—for as long as she could remember. "I don't think that makes me a horrible person."

"No, it doesn't." He started the Cruiser and pulled out of the parking area, his face grim. Kayla turned away, staring at the stark landscape. She didn't think of her father much these days, or of any of her family, really. She was sure they seldom thought of her. Since she had refused to work with them in their con games, she had ceased to be useful to them.

Dylan guided the vehicle over the rutted BLM

road to the highway, but instead of turning toward Ranger headquarters or town, he took another road that led south. "Where are you going?" Kayla asked.

"We have a few hours to kill before we have to be back at the camp for their ceremony," he said. "Do you have somewhere you need to be?"

She always had work to do, but it was nothing that wouldn't wait. "No."

"Then there's someone I want you to meet."

THE BLEAKNESS IN Kayla's voice when she spoke of her father made Dylan want to punch something. All his life he had known he could count on his family to be there for him. He knew they loved him as surely as he knew the sun would rise tomorrow, and if he needed anything at all, his parents and siblings would move heaven and earth to help him. Kayla didn't have that kind of reassurance, and knowing that made him sick at heart.

"Where are we going?" she asked again, when he turned onto the narrow county road that formed one boundary of his family's ranch.

"I'm taking you home," he said.

"To your home?"

"Yeah. This is my family's ranch." He gestured to his left, and the rolling pastureland dotted with Angus heifers and calves. They rounded a curve in the road and the main house came into view—a two-story log cabin with a green metal roof. A deep porch

stretched across the front of the house, and assorted
log-sided sheds and other outbuildings dotted the
land around it.

Kayla sat up straighter, her back pressed against
the seat as if she was trying to put as much distance
as possible between herself and the house. "I don't
think we should barge in like this without calling
first," she said.

"This is my home. I don't have to call before I
show up." He guided the Cruiser under the iron archway that proclaimed Holt Cattle Company, and over
the cattle guard, to the parking area under a trio of
tall spruce.

"You live here?" She stared at the house.

He laughed. "I live in a smaller cabin on another
part of the property. But I grew up here. My parents
live here."

They exited the car and a pair of Border collies
shot across the yard to greet them. Kayla bent to run
her hands over their wriggling bodies. "Oh, aren't
you a pretty pair!"

"Their names are Lucy and Desi," Dylan said.

"They're beautiful." She grinned as both dogs
fought for her attention.

"I see you've met our vicious guard dogs!"

They looked up from the dogs as Dylan's parents approached. As was his habit now, Dylan found
himself assessing the older couple. Dad was thin-
ner than he had been before his heart attack three

months ago, and he had a little more gray in his reddish-blond hair, but he looked good. So much better than he had when Dylan had first seen him in the hospital.

The ordeal had aged his mom, too, added a few more lines to her face, but she, too, looked stronger than she had when Dylan first came home. "Mom, Dad, I'd like you to meet Kayla Larimer. Kayla, this is my mom and dad, Nancy and Bud Holt."

Kayla straightened. "It's nice to meet you," she said.

"Good to meet you." Bud offered his hand.

"So nice of Dylan to bring you to see us," his mom added. Dylan could read the unasked question in her eyes. He wasn't one for bringing women around to meet the family.

"I wanted Kayla to see the ranch," he said, an answer he knew wouldn't really satisfy his mother, but she was too polite to demand more information in Kayla's hearing.

"Well, come on in." Bud took Kayla's arm and escorted her toward the house. "Are you from around here?" he asked.

"I live in Montrose. I'm a private detective. Dylan and I are working a case together."

"Are you now?" His dad's sharp, assessing gaze made Dylan feel like the kid who had been caught sneaking out of the house his freshman year of high school.

"Where are you from originally?" Nancy asked.

"Oh, my family moved around a lot when I was growing up," Kayla said. "I love your dogs." She gestured toward the two pups, which had run ahead. "I've always heard how intelligent Border collies are."

"Oh, they're smart, all right," Bud said. "Smart enough to get into all kinds of trouble if you don't keep them busy."

The four of them mounted the porch. At the top of the steps, Kayla turned to look out across the yard, and at the snow-capped mountains beyond. "What a gorgeous view," she said.

"Yes. I never get tired of the view," Bud said. "This country has a way of growing on people, I think. Pulling them back when they try to leave."

This last comment was for Dylan's benefit, he knew. "I missed all of this while I was in Denver," he said. "I'm glad to be back."

"And we're glad to have you back," his mother said. "Now come, sit down." She gestured toward the grouping of chairs on the porch. "Can I get you something to drink?"

"No, thank you." Kayla perched on the edge of one of the oak rockers lined up against the front wall of the house. Dylan took the chair next to her, while his parents chose the adjacent swing that hung from the porch beams.

"What kind of case are you working on?" Bud asked. "Or can't you say?"

"We're investigating some goings-on that might be related to a group that's been camping in the Curecanti Wilderness Area," Dylan said. "Followers of a man who calls himself the Prophet."

Bud nodded. "I heard a little about them. Sam Wilson ran into a bunch of the women at the farmers' market last Friday. They bought a lot of his produce. He said they seemed nice. Are they causing trouble?"

"We're not sure. Let's just say some things have aroused our suspicions."

Bud rested his arm along the back of the swing and gave it a gentle nudge with the toe of his boot. "There's always a few of these types who take to the wilderness," he said. "Back-to-the-landers or survivalists or religious zealots looking for a better way. Most of them peter out after a while when people find out how tough it really is to live without modern conveniences like indoor plumbing, refrigeration and heat."

"There was a group that passed through here in the seventies," Nancy said. "The rainbow people, or something like that. A bunch of hippies who said they were all for peace and love, but all they really did was sponge off anyone they could, do drugs and leave a mess behind. Bart Tillaman had to take his front-end loader out to the campsite after they left and haul off two or three Dumpsters full of garbage."

"We won't let things go that far," Dylan said. "That's why we're keeping an eye on them."

"And you're helping the Rangers with their investigations?" Nancy asked Kayla.

She looked up from petting the dogs, who had settled on either side of her. "A client hired me to find his daughter," she said. "She's living with this group."

"Those poor parents." Nancy shook her head. "I can't imagine having one of my children run off like that, having to hire a private investigator to track them down."

"You don't have to worry about that," Dylan said.

"No. Especially now that all three of you are living on the ranch." She smiled at Kayla. "Do your parents live near here?"

"I don't have any close family anymore," Kayla said. She shot Dylan a warning look. As if she had to warn him not to air her private business for his parents.

"I'm sorry to hear that," Nancy said. "But a small town can be a good place to be when you're alone in the world. Stay here long enough and people will be treating you like family."

"Which is another way of saying they'll want to know all your business," Dylan said, but he winked to let his mom know he was only teasing—sort of.

"Speaking of family business..." Bud put his hands on his knees and leaned toward Dylan. "I hope you plan on being at the Cattleman's Club meeting next week."

"I don't know, Dad. Work is taking a lot of my time." The monthly meetings of representatives from all the local ranches had never struck him as very productive.

"The board is really trying to get some of the younger members of local ranching families involved," Bud said. "And you could learn a lot about the way the cattle business works in this part of the state."

"All right. I'll be there if I can." One of the reasons he had returned to the ranch was to take on more of the responsibility of running cattle operations, to ease the burden on his parents. And he knew his dad got a kick out of showing off his son, the cop.

"Private investigation must be interesting work," Nancy said, once more including Kayla in the conversation. "I would think a woman would have an advantage in that field."

"Why do you say that?" Bud asked. "Because women are nosier than men?"

Nancy gave her husband a scolding look. "No. Because criminals would be less likely to suspect a woman—especially one who is so young and pretty."

Kayla shifted, clearly uncomfortable. "I've always enjoyed solving puzzles," she said. "And I like working alone and being my own boss."

"I'd love to hear more about it," Nancy said. She

turned to Dylan. "I hope you're planning to stay for dinner."

"Oh, I don't know—" Kayla began.

"We don't have to be back at the camp until dusk," Dylan interrupted. "Might as well not go on an empty stomach."

"We'll grill steaks," Bud said. "Some of our own beef."

"And a salad from the garden," Nancy said.

"Right. The doctor says I've got to eat my vegetables." Bud grinned. "Say you'll stay."

Kayla nodded, and even managed a small smile of her own. "All right."

Nancy stood, and the others rose also. "While I'm cooking, Dylan can give you a tour of the ranch," she said.

Chapter Nine

Kayla eyed the horse, swallowing her trepidation. The animal was considerably taller than her, with a lot more teeth. "I've never ridden a horse before," she said.

"Sunset is an easy mount." Dylan moved alongside her, so close she could feel the heat of him, which sent a corresponding warmth through her. "I'll be right with you, so you don't have anything to worry about."

"Couldn't we drive? Or take an ATV?" She looked longingly toward a trio of all-terrain vehicles parked outside the barn.

"Horseback is the best way to see the place," he said. "Besides, my horse, Bravo, needs exercise. It's been a few days since I rode him. We won't go far, I promise."

The horse snorted and tossed his head. "I don't think he agrees with you," she said. She took a step back, which sent her stumbling into Dylan. His arms encircled her, steadying her. The hard planes and bunched muscles that defined him as so very male stirred something deep in her female core and she stared up at him, lips parted, breathing grown shallow, bracing herself against the flood of longing that weakened her knees.

His eyes locked onto hers, then darkened, and his arms tightened around her. He bent his head, hesitating a fraction of a second with his mouth near hers. Impatient, she slid her hand to the back of his neck and pulled him down.

His mouth was warm and agile, caressing her lips and sending liquid heat through her. He angled his head to deepen the kiss, the brim of his Stetson brushing the top of her hair, the faint afternoon shadow of his beard a pleasant friction against her skin.

When at last he raised his head, she blinked up at him, trying to clear away the fog of lust. "Wh-why did you do that?" she stammered.

"Because you wanted me to. And because I wanted to." He patted the horse's neck. "It stopped you from being afraid of Sunset, didn't it?"

Wishing to deny both the accusation that she had wanted him to kiss her and that she had been afraid of the horse, but knowing she wasn't that accomplished a liar, she turned away him and stuck her foot in the stirrup. "Let's get go—"

Before she could complete the sentence, he had moved to boost her onto the horse, the feel of his hand against the seat of her jeans staying with her even when she was settled in the saddle. He handed her the reins. "Don't jerk on them," he said. "Mostly, Sunset will follow Bravo. You just relax and enjoy the scenery."

That scenery included Dylan on horseback as he rode ahead of her down a trail that led away from the house. He sat relaxed in the saddle, tall and broad-shouldered, his Stetson cocked just-so on his head. What had possessed her to kiss the man like that? The move was unprofessional and impulsive and probably a lot of other things that in no way described her.

For the next half hour she followed him down the trail. He pointed out various outbuildings and pastures, and talked about some of the livestock and the history of the ranch. "My great-grandfather bought the land during the Depression, when it cost next to nothing. He worked for years adding to it and building it up to make it what it is today." Kayla heard the pride in Dylan's voice and felt a stab of jealousy. What would it be like to feel so connected to a place? To the land?

He stopped at the top of a hill that afforded a vista of a sweeping river valley. "Our place extends to the base of those hills over there," he said, pointing.

"It's beautiful." Unlike the almost barren terrain near the national park, this valley was green, and dotted with small herds of cattle that grazed in the knee-high grass. She glanced at Dylan. He was looking out across the landscape, fine lines spreading at the corners of his eyes as he squinted in the brightness, his lips curved in a half smile. "Did you enjoy growing up here?" she asked.

"I did. I liked to ride and shoot and fish, and being outdoors." He shifted, the saddle creaking as he half turned toward her. "But when I got to be a teenager, I grew restless. I was interested in a career in law enforcement and I didn't see much chance for advancement here. It's a pretty small police department, and there wasn't anything like the Ranger Brigade back then."

"So you went to Denver."

"Yes. And I liked it. The city is a good place to be if you're a single, twentysomething guy. And it was good for my career."

"But you came back."

"My folks needed me. And it was time. As much as I enjoyed Denver, it wasn't the kind of place I could picture myself raising a family."

"You really think about things like that—raising a family?"

"Don't you?"

She shook her head. "No." The idea unsettled her a little. She was happy being responsible for herself, but she didn't need to be responsible for anyone else.

"Maybe that's why Andi Matheson hooked up with Metwater's group," Dylan said. "Maybe she thought that kind of makeshift family would be a good place to raise a kid."

"It sounds like a terrible idea." Kayla's own childhood had been defined by constantly moving around with an ever-shifting group of her father's followers. "What I can't figure is what Daniel Metwater gets out of it."

"A power trip? A bunch of devoted, beautiful women? Or maybe he's looking for a family of his own." Dylan turned his horse and led the way back down the hill. At the bottom the trail widened, so they could ride side by side.

True to Dylan's word, Sunset was an easygoing mount that was content to follow Dylan's horse's lead. Kayla was able to relax and focus away from her own fears and annoyances to the case. "From what I've read, he comes from money," she said. "Why give that up to live in the desert?"

"He thinks he's a prophet. It's his calling."

"Or he's running away from something."

"Or that." Dylan glanced at her. "Anything in particular make you think so?"

"When my father ran into trouble and needed to leave a place, he would always announce that he had had a vision—God leading him to take his message to new, more fertile fields."

Dylan nodded. "You've given me an idea."

"What's that?"

"I'm going to dig a little deeper into Metwater's

background. Maybe I'll find something there that will help in this investigation. Some secret he's not keen to have revealed."

THE SUN WAS sinking behind the distant hills when Dylan and Kayla finally left the ranch. Dinner had been a leisurely affair on the back deck of his parents' home—steaks grilled outdoors, served with roasted corn and an enormous salad of fresh greens and tomatoes from his mother's garden.

Kayla had seemed to enjoy herself and Dylan had enjoyed watching her. His lips still warmed at the memory of that impulsive kiss. Maybe not the most professional move he had ever pulled, but he'd been thinking about kissing her practically since they met. When she had pulled his mouth down to hers he hadn't been about to resist. He had enjoyed the kiss very much, and he enjoyed knowing that he'd been able to breach her reserve. She had made it clear she didn't trust anyone—and maybe she had good reason for that, given what little he knew of her upbringing. But that kiss told him that maybe she was beginning to have more faith in him, at least a bit.

He braked to avoid a deer that darted across the road in the graying light. "It's going to be dark by the time we get to the camp," Kayla said.

"Probably." He switched on the Cruiser's head-lights. "Maybe they'll think we skipped out on their invitation. I don't mind catching them off guard."

She crossed her arms over her chest. "Nothing about this feels right. Why do you think Metwater invited us to this ceremony?"

"He said it was to help us understand the Family more."

"I don't believe him."

"I'm not sure I do, either, but I want to know what he's up to. Why don't you believe him?"

"Because people like him aren't altruistic. I doubt he cares if we understand him and his group or not. He thrives on manipulating people. I can't help but think he's trying to manipulate *us*."

"We're not going to let him do that, are we?"

"Nobody manipulates me."

When he glanced over, she had her gaze fixed on him. Dylan wondered if her words were a not-so-subtle warning. He could have protested that he wasn't the manipulative type, but better she learn that fact for herself.

Light from an almost full moon bathed the wilderness landscape in silver, highlighting the rocky hoodoos and cliffs, and sending long shadows across the sparse grass. A coyote trotted down the road ahead, turning to regard them with golden eyes before darting into the underbrush. "I can't believe anyone would want to live out here," Kayla said. "It's so…desolate."

"It would be a tough place to live," Dylan agreed. "But it's a good place to hide." He found the parking area and pulled in and shut off the engine. Silence closed around them like a muffling blanket, the only sound the faint ticking of the cooling motor. Though the moon provided plenty of illumination, Dylan tucked a mini Maglite into his pocket just in case. They climbed out of the Cruiser and looked around.

"Metwater said he would have someone waiting for us, but I don't see anyone," Kayla said.

"Maybe he thinks we're not going to show." Dylan touched her arm. "Come on. Let's slip in quietly and see what they're up to."

They moved up the path toward the camp, placing their footsteps carefully, trying not to disturb the night's silence. As they rounded the outcropping of rock that guarded the entrance to the camp, they heard a low murmuring. Dylan stopped to listen and Kayla moved up beside him. "What's that?" he whispered.

"Sounds like some kind of chanting or something," she said.

He nodded, and led the way around the outcropping. No guards watched over the entrance to the camp—apparently everyone was gathered around the bonfire in the center of the circle of trailers and tents. The faces of everyone—men, women and children— were fixed on the leaping flames, and voices rose in unison. "In unity is power. Power is unity."

Power to do what? "Doesn't sound like a peaceful manifesto to me," Dylan muttered. "And there's a burn ban on. Want to bet they don't have a permit for that fire?"

Kayla shushed him as Daniel Metwater stepped from the crowd and stood in front of the blaze, his profile to Dylan and Kayla. The crowd fell silent as he waited. He was naked except for a loincloth, his body gleaming in the firelight as if it had been oiled. He was thin but muscular, and wore the expression of a man who was confident he was right.

Two women moved from the crowd to join him. They were dressed only in loincloths also, their breasts painted with red and black concentric circles, their eyes ringed in black, lips outlined in red. Dylan didn't recognize either of them, but they fit the profile of twentysomething beauties predominant among Metwater's followers.

A drum began a slow, steady beat, gradually increasing in tempo. Metwater extended his arms and the women took his hands. The three began a slow, hypnotic dance, swaying and writhing around each other. Beside him, Kayla shifted. "Do you think he invited us to watch an orgy?" she asked.

"Maybe he wanted us to join in."

She sent him a sour look and he bit back a grin. Then he had a sudden image of her dressed in only a loincloth and he had to look away. He forced his mind back to the business at hand. "Let's wait a bit more and see what happens before we announce ourselves," he said.

The drums stopped and the two women took seats on either side of the circle. Metwater held up his hands to silence the crowd. "Tonight marks a very special night." His voice carried easily in the still night air, with the rounded tones and precise diction of an experienced orator. Those gathered around the fire listened raptly, eyes glowing, some with lips slightly parted.

"We gather under the light of the full moon to welcome a new member to our family." He continued with a flowery speech about the sacredness of family, the importance of connection and generally how superior they all were for having made the decision to join up with the Prophet. "Ours is a sacred bond of mind, body and spirit," he proclaimed. "We are united mentally, physically and in our souls. It is a union of our most sacred natures, and of our blood."

At this last, he pulled a large dagger from a sheath at his side and sliced the blade across his own palm. Kayla gasped, and Dylan put out a hand to restrain her.

Metwater turned away from them, toward the far side of the circle. "We begin, as always, with the sacrifice," he said.

Two men—Dylan thought he recognized Abe and Zach beneath the black-and-white greasepaint that streaked their faces—escorted a young woman to the center of the circle. She wore a long white robe, and her dark hair fell almost to her waist. Her face was ivory white in the moonlight, the flames reflecting in her glassy eyes.

Metwater kissed each of her cheeks in turn, then motioned for her to kneel. He held the dagger over his head, the blade still wet with his own blood, firelight glinting off the steel. "Persephone, you have agreed to sacrifice what is necessary to make our family whole," he intoned. Then he brought the blade down to rest at her throat.

Dylan didn't have to see any more. He drew his weapon and charged forward, Kayla at his heels. "Stop!" he shouted. "Drop the knife and step back with your hands up."

Chapter Ten

Kayla's heart pounded in rhythm with her racing feet as she followed Dylan toward the macabre scene around the fire. Daniel Metwater, blood dripping from the palm of one hand as he gripped the dagger with the other, turned toward them as the girl slumped to the ground beside him. The crowd of followers around the blaze stared, but none made a move as Dylan stopped and trained his gun on Metwater. "Drop the knife," he ordered.

Metwater opened his hand and let the knife fall. Kayla moved to the young woman and checked her pulse, which was strong. She moaned a little and stirred, and Kayla helped her sit up. "It's okay," she soothed. "You're okay."

"Put that gun away now, Officer!" Metwater's face glowed red in the firelight. "I invited you here tonight to witness the ceremony, not to disrupt it."

Dylan didn't waver. "Put your hands behind your back and turn around," he said. "You're under arrest."

"On what charge?" Metwater continued to glare at Dylan.

"For the attempted murder of that young woman." He nodded toward the woman who sat beside Kayla.

Metwater's laughter was loud and raucous. Others in the crowd joined him in the mocking mirth. Anger tightened Kayla's throat, and she read the same rage in Dylan's eyes. Keeping his gaze fixed on Metwater, Dylan addressed the young woman. "Ma'am, are you all right?"

"I'm fine." Now that she had recovered consciousness, Persephone—or whatever her real name was— seemed fine, a little pale maybe, but perfectly calm.

"Of course she's fine," Metwater said. "This was a ceremony, not a murder. Haven't you heard of symbolism, Lieutenant?" He moved to the young woman's side and helped her to her feet. Kayla could smell the sweat and blood on him, odors that made him seem even more primitive and wild. "Persephone and I were acting out the symbolic death of her old self. In the next phase, you would have seen her reborn into her new life with the Family."

Kayla became aware of others in the crowd moving closer. Out of the corner of her eyes, she spotted the two men who had served as Persephone's escorts moving around to flank her.

"Tell your guards to move back," Dylan said.

Metwater flicked his gaze toward the men. "Put

away your gun. Your threat of violence has tainted our sacred proceedings."

Dylan holstered his weapon. Kayla joined him, anxious to put more distance between herself and Metwater. "You're one to talk of violence," she told him. "Considering you're bleeding all over the place."

Metwater studied his bleeding palm. "Every member of the Family has some of my blood mixed in their veins," he said. "Symbolizing that I am the father and protector of all."

Kayla wrinkled her nose, but said nothing.

"The ceremony is over." Dylan raised his voice to be heard by the crowd. "Go on back to your camps."

"The ceremony isn't over until I say it's over." Metwater handed Persephone off to one of the half-naked women he had danced with and started toward Dylan.

Kayla stiffened, and wished she'd brought her gun with her. If Dylan needed backup, she wasn't going to be of much use.

"Don't argue with me, Metwater," Dylan said. "I could still take you in for questioning."

"Questioning about what?"

"The murder of Special Agent Frank Asher, for one," Dylan said.

"I told you, I had nothing to do with Agent Asher's death."

"You and your followers are the only ones around,"

Dylan said. "Asher came here, probably to talk to Andi Matheson, possibly to try to talk her into leaving your group. Maybe you shot him in order to prevent that. Or maybe Asher had uncovered your secret, and you couldn't risk him exposing you."

"What secret? I don't have a secret." But fear flashed in Metwater's dark eyes, though the rest of his expression remained stony.

"Don't you?" Dylan turned to the young woman. "What's your real name?" he asked.

"P-Priscilla," she said. "Priscilla Ortega."

"How old are you, Priscilla?"

"I'm nineteen."

"Enough questions." Metwater stepped between them. "Persephone has done nothing wrong." He motioned for the dancer to take the younger woman away and she did so. "You need to leave now also, Officer." He glanced at Kayla. "You may stay if you like, Miss Larimer."

Kayla didn't try to hide her disgust at the invitation. "I'm not one of your brainwashed devotees," she said.

"I'm going to remind you again that you're on public land," Dylan said.

Metwater folded his arms across his muscular chest and met Dylan's stern gaze. "This is our home, Officer. And you're not welcome here." With that, he turned his back on Dylan and stalked toward his trailer.

"Somebody put out this fire," Dylan called after him. "There's a burn ban on for the county."

Metwater raised one hand to indicate he had heard.

"I'm going to find out your secret," Dylan called. "And when I do, I'm going to tell all your followers the kind of man you really are."

Metwater stumbled, then caught himself and kept walking. But Kayla knew Dylan's words had gotten to the man. Daniel Metwater was definitely guilty of something. Whether his crime was murder or something else, Kayla intended to help expose him sooner rather than later.

KAYLA SHIVERED AND wrapped her arms around her shoulders, then leaned forward to punch up the blower on the heater in Dylan's Cruiser as they left the wilderness area and turned onto the paved highway leading back to Montrose. "I can't get that girl's face out of my mind," she said. "When Metwater held that knife to her throat, she was absolutely terrified. She believed he was going to kill her, no matter what he told us."

Dylan said nothing, but continued to stare out the windshield, both hands gripping the steering wheel, his body tense. "Well?" she prompted. "What do you think? Do you think he was really going to slit her throat?"

"I've been thinking about what you said earlier," he said.

"What I said?" She blinked. "What did I say?"

"That Metwater is trying to manipulate us."

"Of course he is. That's how people like him operate—how they keep control of any group of people or situation. He— Oh?" Dylan's meaning hit her. "Are you saying he staged that whole business with the knife and the so-called sacrifice for our benefit? That he wanted us to see it?"

"I don't know. But replaying everything in my mind, I think he knew we were standing there from the moment we arrived. And he must have ordered his bodyguards not to make a move, or they would have been on us like a shot."

"But why? So we would think he was capable of murder?" She shook her head. "That's twisted even for a guy who calls himself a prophet."

"Maybe he wanted us to look like a couple of idiots in front of his followers," Dylan said. "Or maybe it's sleight of hand—get us to focus on the perceived human sacrifice so we don't notice something else that's going on."

"So, what else is going on?" She turned down the heater, warmer at last as anger replaced some of her earlier shock. "I can't believe he didn't have something to do with Frank Asher's murder, but he's got a whole camp full of followers who will no doubt swear he was with all of them the morning Frank was shot."

"He could have ordered the hit."

"He could have. But good luck proving that."

"I'm going to do some more digging into his background and see what I come up with."

"Will you let me know what you find?" She leaned toward him, cutting off the objection she was sure he was about to make. "I'm in this with you right up to my ears," she said. "You can't cut me off now. And until Senator Matheson tells me otherwise, I'm still concerned about Andi. I have to figure out how involved she is in all of this."

"When I checked in with headquarters earlier, there was still no sign of the senator," Dylan said.

"How could a man in the public eye like the senator just disappear?" she asked. "Do the police think he was kidnapped—or killed?"

"There weren't any signs of foul play," Dylan said. "Maybe he just decided to take a break from public life. There isn't a law against that."

"Except that Senator Matheson thrives on being in the public eye. I read an article that listed him as one of the most media-savvy politicians."

"So maybe this is some kind of publicity stunt—disappear for a while to get people talking, then show up again."

"And say what—'surprise, I fooled you'?"

"He could say he'd been on a secret fact-finding

mission or something. For all we know, he's in Mexico or the Caribbean right now, relaxing on the beach while we waste resources searching for him. Metwater isn't the only manipulator we're dealing with here, I think."

"Maybe." But something about that scenario bothered her. She searched for the words to voice her impressions of the senator. "He was waiting for me to give him my report about Andi. When he hired me, he seemed very anxious to know that she was all right. If he did plan to disappear as some kind of publicity stunt or ploy for attention, it doesn't make sense that he would do so before he heard back from me."

"Was he really concerned, or was he only pretending for your benefit?" Dylan asked.

"I think his worry was genuine." But how could she be sure? She shifted in her seat. "I haven't had that much personal experience with genuine parental devotion, but I'm pretty good at spotting fake emotions. All his pomposity and bombast softened when Senator Matheson spoke about his daughter. He talked a lot about how he had tried all his life to protect her and do what was best for her. How if only she would come back to him, he could give her everything she needed and deserved."

"That kind of love can be smothering to some people—especially a person Andi's age, who is trying to exert her independence."

Kayla nodded. "He said it would be enough to

know she was safe, but I had the feeling that once I located her, he would try everything in his power to persuade her to return to him. Which is another reason I can't believe he would voluntarily disappear before he was sure of her safety."

"That investigation is out of our hands," Dylan said. "We have to worry about things closer to home. I'm going to do more digging into Frank Asher's and Daniel Metwater's backgrounds tomorrow."

"Hmm." She'd be doing the same, but there was no point telling him and hearing a lecture about not interfering in police business.

"If you find out anything interesting about either of them, I hope you'll share it with me," Dylan said.

She felt her face heat, and was grateful he couldn't see the flush in the darkness. "I might. If you'll do the same with me."

"Even twelve hours ago I probably would have said no, but I'm beginning to think the two of us make a great team and we'll accomplish more working together than at cross purposes."

This admission surprised her. "What changed your mind?"

"You did great back at the camp just now—and earlier today when we spoke with Andi and Metwater. You've got a cool head and good instincts, and I trust you to watch my back."

She fought back the surge of emotion that tightened her throat. Dylan didn't strike her as the type of person to throw around words like that casually. "Thank you," she managed to squeeze out.

"I hope you'll come to trust me," he said.

She rubbed a hand up and down her thigh. "I'm used to working alone." Depending on other people was too risky.

"I think the two of us make a good team," he said again. He cleared his throat. "I'd like to see more of you."

"I'll stay in touch. I want to know what you find out about Metwater and the rest."

"I meant after this case is resolved. I liked kissing you this afternoon. I'd like to do it again."

Her breath caught and her heart pounded, the memory of his lips on hers and his arms around her leaving her with the same warm, weak-kneed sensation that had overwhelmed her in the barn. "That was a mistake," she said.

"Why do you say that? I got the impression you enjoyed it, too," he said.

Yes, she had enjoyed kissing Dylan. More than she had enjoyed anything in a long while. But letting him get that close to her would only bring trouble. "I don't do relationships," she said. "I'm not good at them." No matter how promising things started, other people always let you down. Maybe that was part of being human, but she couldn't risk any more betrayals. Other people might be good at forgiving, but she wasn't.

"I think you underestimate yourself," he said. "Or maybe you underestimate me. I'm willing to take things slow."

She shook her head, then realized he might not be able to see her. "No. You're a great guy, but I prefer to keep things between us professional."

"So no more kisses?"

"No more." She had to hold back a sigh. The kiss really had been great, but kissing Dylan again would only lead to more kissing and hugging and caressing and… She shoved the thoughts away and sat up straighter. They were almost to the turnoff for her house. She wouldn't have to see Dylan again for a couple of days at least, and that time would allow her emotions to cool off and settle. When he had time to think about it, he would see the sense in keeping his distance from her, as well.

He switched on his blinker to make the left turn, waiting for an approaching car to pass. Behind them, headlights glowed in the distance. Kayla squinted and shielded her eyes from the glare in the side mirror. What was the guy behind them doing with his brights up? And he was driving awfully fast, wasn't he?

The car approaching in the opposite lane passed and Dylan took his foot off the brake, prepared to make the turn. But before he could act, the car behind them slammed into them, clipping the back bumper and sending the Cruiser spinning off the

FREE Merchandise is 'in the Cards' for you!

Dear Reader,

We're giving away FREE MERCHANDISE!

Seriously, we'd like to reward you for reading this novel by giving you **FREE MERCHANDISE** worth over $20 retail. And no purchase is necessary!

You see the Jack of Hearts sticker above? Paste that sticker in the box on the Free Merchandise Voucher inside. Return the Voucher today... and we'll send you Free Merchandise!

Thanks again for reading one of our novels—and enjoy your Free Merchandise with our compliments!

Pam Powers

Pam Powers

P.S. Look inside to see what Free Merchandise is **"in the cards"** for you!

W

e'd like to send you two free books like the one you are enjoying now. Your two books have a combined cover price of over $10 retail, but they are yours to keep absolutely FREE! We'll even send you 2 wonderful surprise gifts. You can't lose!

REMEMBER: Your Free Merchandise, consisting of **2 Free Books** and **2 Free Gifts**, is worth over $20 retail! No purchase is necessary, so please send for your Free Merchandise today.

Get TWO FREE GIFTS!

We'll also send you 2 wonderful FREE GIFTS (worth about $10 retail), in addition to your 2 Free books!

YOUR FREE MERCHANDISE INCLUDES...
2 FREE Books **AND** 2 FREE Mystery Gifts

FREE MERCHANDISE VOUCHER

2 FREE BOOKS and 2 FREE GIFTS

Please send my Free Merchandise, consisting of
2 Free Books and **2 Free Mystery Gifts**.
I understand that I am under no obligation to buy
anything, as explained on the back of this card.

❏ I prefer the regular-print edition
182/382 HDL GLTE

❏ I prefer the larger-print edition
199/399 HDL GLTE

Please Print

FIRST NAME

LAST NAME

ADDRESS

APT.#   CITY

STATE/PROV.   ZIP/POSTAL CODE

Offer limited to one per household and not applicable to series that subscriber is currently receiving.
Your Privacy—The Reader Service is committed to protecting your privacy. Our Privacy Policy is available online at www.ReaderService.com or upon request from the Reader Service. We make a portion of our mailing list available to reputable third parties that offer products we believe may interest you. If you prefer that we not exchange your name with third parties, or if you wish to clarify or modify your communication preferences, please visit us at www.ReaderService.com/consumerschoice or write to us at Reader Service Preference Service, P.O. Box 9062, Buffalo, NY 14240-9062. Include your complete name and address.

NO PURCHASE NECESSARY!

HI-517-FMIVY17

(left margin, vertical text)

▲ Detach card and mail today. No stamp needed. ▲

® and ™ are trademarks owned and used by the trademark owner and/or its licensee. Printed in the U.S.A.
© 2016 HARLEQUIN ENTERPRISES LIMITED.

road and into the ditch. The air bags exploded, pressing Kayla back against the seat. Then she heard another sound—the metallic pop of bullets striking metal as someone fired into their vehicle.

Chapter Eleven

Dylan woke to flashing lights and the distant wail of a siren. Pain stabbed at his skull and he realized he was tilted at an odd angle. He blinked, trying to get his bearings. Something about asking Kayla to kiss him. Or telling her he wanted to kiss her… No, that wasn't it.

"Dylan? Dylan, are you okay?" Kayla's voice, strained with anxiety, cut through the fog in his head.

"I'm okay." He tried to shift his body and realized he was sandwiched between the expanded air bag and the back of his seat. "What happened?"

"A car, or maybe a truck, plowed into us from behind. I think they did it deliberately. And I thought I heard gunshots. Are you sure you're okay?"

He felt his head. No blood there, though he must have hit it against the side of the car when they crashed. "I'm fine. What about you? Are you all right?"

"A little banged up, but nothing broken. My door is wedged into the ditch, so I can't open it."

He felt at his side for his phone and dragged it out of its holster. "I'll call for help."

"I think someone's coming. I hear a siren."

The sound was getting closer, but the flashing lights were his own. He must have bumped the control during the crash.

Moments later, two emergency vehicles arrived, followed by a third. Red-and-blue lights strobed across the darkness, and moments later the beam of a flashlight played across Dylan's face. He winced and shielded his eyes from the light as someone yanked open his door.

"Don't try to move," the responding officer said. "Not until the paramedic has checked you out."

"I think I just have a bump on the head." Dylan shoved his phone back into its holster. There would be time enough later to call the captain.

"You part of the Ranger Brigade?" the officer asked, glancing at the logo on the side of the Cruiser.

"Yes. Lieutenant Dylan Holt with the Colorado State Patrol."

A paramedic, young with a dark goatee, joined the officer, directing his flashlight beam over Dylan and Kayla. "How are you doing, miss?" he asked.

"I'm okay," she said. "Just a little shaken up, and I can't get out of the car."

"We'll help you in just a minute." The paramedic turned to Dylan. "Any pain or obvious injuries?"

"Just my head." He touched the knot on his forehead. "Nothing broken."

"You climb out then, and we'll see about getting to your passenger."

Dylan climbed out of the car, the officer and a second paramedic helping. They led him to an ambulance, where he submitted to an examination.

"What happened?" the officer, a middle-aged African American whose badge identified him as Officer Lejeune, asked.

Dylan took a moment to organize his thoughts, though most of his initial fog had cleared. "I was stopped, waiting to make a left turn, when a vehicle plowed into me from behind," he said. He kept his gaze on the Cruiser, where the first paramedic and another officer were helping Kayla climb out. "The other vehicle clipped my back bumper and we spun out of control. I hit my head and must have been out for a minute. Maybe a little longer."

"So whoever hit you fled the scene?" Officer Lejeune asked.

"I guess so." He thought about what Kayla had said—about hearing shots fired. If that was true, why hadn't whoever had targeted them stayed around to finish the job?

"Another driver called it in," Lejeune said. "She said the other vehicle was speeding and plowed right into you, then sped away."

"Did she mention any gunshots?" Dylan asked.

Lejeune and the paramedic exchanged glances. "Gunshots?"

"Someone was firing at us. I'm sure that's what I heard." Kayla limped toward them, moving ahead of the men supporting her.

Dylan shoved aside the paramedic, who was trying to apply an ice pack to the knot on his head, and hurried to her. "You're hurt," he said.

"I just banged my knee. I'll be fine." But she didn't push him away and leaned into him when he put his arm around her.

"I'll take a look at the car," Lejeune said, and strode off.

Dylan escorted Kayla to the ambulance and sat beside her as the paramedic bent to examine her knee. "Did you get a good look at the vehicle that hit us?" he asked.

"No. The brights were on—though I had the impression it was big. Maybe a pickup truck or a big SUV?" She shook her head. "It happened so fast."

The two police officers returned. "We found what could be bullet holes in the driver's-side door," Lejeune said. "Small caliber."

"You're lucky whoever ran you down didn't have a bigger gun or wasn't a better shot," the second officer, Raybourn, said.

"Whoever it was, I don't think they were trying to kill us," Dylan said. "They wanted to scare us."

"They scared me," Kayla admitted. "But they also made me mad. I never have liked bullies."

"You think this has to do with a case you're investigating?" Lejeune asked.

"Maybe." Dylan pulled out his phone again. "I'm going to get someone from my team to check out the Cruiser, see what we can find."

He stepped away to make his call while the paramedics finished checking Kayla. His stomach churned as he stared at the car on its side in the ditch, the back end smashed.

Graham answered on the fourth ring. "Hello, Lieutenant," he said, as calm and alert as if the call had come at midday, instead of after ten at night.

"Kayla Larimer and I were on our way back to town from Daniel Metwater's camp and someone ran us off the road," Dylan said. "They took a couple of shots at us, too."

"Are you all right?" Graham asked, his voice sharper. "Is Kayla all right?"

"We're a little banged up, but okay. I'd like a team to come check out the Cruiser and the area, see if we can come up with any clues."

"We'll send someone. Did you get a look at who did this?"

"No. A woman called in the accident, but it

doesn't sound like she got a good look, either, though we'll want to talk to her."

"Do you think it was one of Metwater's followers?"

"Maybe." The hit-and-run was the kind of impulsive lashing out he might expect from the mostly young members of the group, but Metwater himself didn't strike him as that sloppy.

"What were you doing at his camp?" Graham asked.

"He invited us, actually, to observe some kind of ceremony." Dylan rubbed his throbbing head. "I'll give you my report later. Right now, I need to see about getting Kayla home. Then I'll wait here with the Cruiser."

"I'll have someone out there as soon as I can. If we find anything that links this to Metwater's group, you can be sure we'll be hauling them all in for questioning."

Dylan ended the call and stowed the phone, then walked back to Kayla. "I'll find someone to give you a ride home," he said. "I need to wait here."

"Officer Raybourn has already offered me a ride." She rested her hand on Dylan's arm. "Are you sure you're okay? That knot on your head looks like it hurts."

He gingerly touched the swelling. "I'll be okay. My dad always did say I had a hard head."

"I liked your parents," she said. "I forgot to thank you for taking me to meet them. I really enjoyed it."

"I enjoyed it, too." He rested his palm on her shoulder, giving her the chance to pull away, but hoping she wouldn't. "You're welcome to visit anytime."

"Hmm." She looked down, but didn't shift away or remove her hand from his arm. "I'm glad you weren't seriously hurt," she said. "When I first called your name and you didn't answer..." She let her voice trail away.

"I know. I'm glad you're not hurt, too." He brought his hand up to cup the side of her face, then bent and kissed her—just a gentle brush of his lips across hers. She let out a sigh and leaned into him, returning the kiss for a brief moment before pulling away.

"I'm not sure how to handle you," she said. "I'd better go." She turned away and hurried toward where Raybourn and Lejeune waited.

"You're doing a fine job so far," Dylan said softly.

EVERYTHING ACHED WHEN Kayla woke the next morning. She dragged herself into a hot shower, then chased two ibuprofen with a cup of strong tea. She was still sore, but felt able to get to work. She headed to the spare room that served as her home office and flipped through the mail that had accumulated in the last few days. She had been so busy dealing with Senator Matheson and Andi that she hadn't gotten around to reading it.

An envelope from the Colorado Private Investigators Society caught her attention and she slit it open, then unfolded the single sheet of heavy cream-colored paper inside.

Dear Ms. Larimer,

We are pleased to inform you that you have been selected as this year's Western Slope Private Investigator of the Year. You will be one of the honorees at the Colorado Western Region Honors Banquet in Grand Junction on August 23.

Please RSVP to the email address below and indicate if you will be bringing a guest.

Congratulations on your honor,
Madeline Zimeski, President

Kayla stared at the letter, annoyed. She hadn't even known there was a Western Slope Private Investigator of the Year. Who had nominated her? And she had to attend a banquet. Did this mean she'd have to buy a fancy dress? And shoes?

She put the letter aside and forced herself to work on a background check for a legal firm she did small jobs for, then started on a report on some surveillance she'd done on a straying husband the week before. But her mind kept straying back to Andi Matheson, the missing senator and enigmatic Daniel Metwater.

The image of him, almost naked and gleaming in the firelight, blood dripping from his hands as he held the dagger to that young woman's throat, would stay with her for a long time, she imagined. Being around him put her on edge, maybe because he reminded her too much of her own father—handsome and charismatic, good at reading people and promising them what they wanted, or exploiting their weaknesses.

What weakness had he exploited in Andi? Maybe he had painted a picture of the Family as a safe refuge in which she could raise her baby. On his side, he had a recruit with money. At twenty-four, Andi had her own funds. Had she signed them over to Metwater? Or maybe the Prophet merely liked having a senator's daughter in his retinue. Could Metwater be linked to the senator's disappearance?

She jotted these questions into a notebook she kept open on her desk, then pulled out her phone. Time to do a little more digging.

"Hello?" The young woman on the other end of the line sounded sleepy.

"Tessa? It's Kayla Larimer—the private detective who was trying to find Andi Matheson."

"Oh, uh, hi." Tessa sounded more awake, but wary. "Did you find her?"

"I did. You were right in thinking she'd hooked up with that spiritual group you mentioned—the Family."

"The one with that hot guy, right?" Tessa snorted. "I knew it. That night we met I could tell he was really into her. That was the problem with going anywhere with Andi. All the men ended up looking at her. I might as well have been invisible."

"The hot guy is Daniel Metwater, the leader of the group. He calls himself the Prophet."

Tessa yawned. "I remember now. He talked a lot about personal freedom and connecting with nature and building a true family—Andi ate it all up. I figured he just wanted to get into her pants."

"So Daniel Metwater didn't impress you?" Kayla asked.

"He was really hot, but he knew it. I mean, he had all these women fawning over him and he acted like that was just the way it should be. And all his talk about family and connection and everything didn't do anything for me. I already have a family, and the whole reason people build houses is to keep nature at a distance, right?"

Kayla smiled. She supposed that was one way to look at it. "Why do you think Andi was so interested in what he had to say?" she asked. "She had a family, too, and what looked like a pretty nice life."

"She had a nice life, but lately she and her dad were on the outs."

"Do you know why she and her father weren't getting along?"

"Oh, the usual—he still treated her like a child,

always trying to tell her what to do and how to act and how to live her life. She hated that. But that wasn't really anything new. The senator was always a little…I'd call it overprotective. I think she even liked it sometimes, how she could crook her little finger and Daddy would come running. I saw on the news about her dad disappearing. Even though they weren't getting along, I'll bet Andi's pretty upset about that."

She hadn't appeared to be, but Kayla didn't bother going into that. "You said Andi and her dad not getting along wasn't anything new, so what was different this time? What made her want to break ties with her father altogether?"

"I'm really not sure. I think it might have had something to do with the guy she was seeing last year."

Kayla sat up straighter. "Who was that?"

"I never met him. Andi said he was an older man, and he worked for her father. It was all very mysterious. I told her I bet he was married, since he never wanted to be seen in public with her. She said it was because her father wouldn't approve, but it turned out I was right."

"You mean the man *was* married?" Kayla asked. No one had mentioned Agent Asher having a wife.

"Kayla told me he had a wife and three kids right here in Denver. She was furious when she found out—but not half as furious as her father. He fired the guy and lit into Andi. She decided she didn't want to have anything to do with either one of them. I think that's one reason this Daniel guy's spiel about getting away from it all and starting over appealed to her. Did she tell you she was pregnant?"

"Yes, she told me."

"So you can't blame her for wanting a better life for her baby—something more peaceful. Is she doing okay with Daniel and his group?"

"She's healthy and she seems content." No sense going into the news of Frank Asher's death.

"I'm glad. If you see her again, tell her I said hi. And thanks for letting me know you found her."

"Sure." That wasn't the reason she had called, but it was okay with her if Tessa thought so.

They said their goodbyes and Kayla ended the call. So Andi hadn't told her and Dylan the whole story about her relationship with Frank Asher. He wasn't just her former lover and the father of her child, but a man who had betrayed her, in a big way. Had he hurt her enough to make her want to hurt him in return?

She stared at her phone, then scrolled to Dylan's number. He answered right away. "Hey," he said. "How are you feeling this morning?"

"Like I've been run over by a truck. How about you?"

"The same. And you're right about it being a truck, or at least we're pretty sure." Wind noise and the muffled rumble of traffic told her he was outside. She pictured him standing on the side of the road by the damaged Cruiser—or maybe back at Ranger Brigade headquarters in the park. "We found some paint scrapes on the Cruiser and they match up to the height of a pickup—probably with one of those heavy-duty brush guards on the front."

"Any idea who was driving?"

"Not yet. But we're going to keep digging. Have you given your statement to the Montrose Police yet?"

"It's on my list for this morning. I told Officers Raybourn and Lejeune I'd stop by."

"It would be good if you could swing by here and give us a formal statement, too. Just in case this turns out to be connected to Metwater and the Family."

"Sure. I could do that." She fought the urge to ask if he would be there. She wanted to see him again, but didn't want to appear too eager. "I've found something else for you to dig into," she said instead.

"Oh? Hang on a minute. Let me get where I can hear you better." She waited while he walked somewhere. She heard a door open and close, then everything was quieter. "Okay, what's up?"

"I talked to Tessa Madigan this morning—Andi's friend who told me about their meeting with Metwater and the Family."

"I remember. You said a friend of hers told you about Andi's interest in Metwater."

"Right. I asked her why Andi wanted to join the group—what had made her so upset she would leave her comfortable life behind. Tessa said she thought it had something to do with the man she had been dating before."

"Frank Asher?"

"Tessa didn't know his name. She said the relationship was very secretive. Turns out there was a good reason for that."

"And are you going to tell me the reason or make me play a game of twenty questions?"

"Patience, Lieutenant. Tessa said the reason Andi and this guy split was because Andi found out he had a wife and three kids in Denver."

Dylan let out a low whistle. "I guess that made her furious. But if that man was Asher, was she angry enough to shoot him and leave him lying in the desert?"

"I have a hard time believing it, considering how big a shock the news seemed to be to her."

"Maybe she's a good actress," Dylan said.

"Or maybe there's another woman you should consider."

He was silent for a moment, then said, "The wife."

"If I found out my husband and the father of our three children was sneaking around with another woman I might want to put an end to the relationship," Kayla said.

"And maybe a permanent end to him," Dylan agreed.

Chapter Twelve

Dylan stepped out to where the techs were finishing their examination of his Cruiser, which they had towed to headquarters from the scene of the accident. Simon walked over to meet him. "We got some chips of the paint," he said, and held out an evidence bag with three black contact-lens-sized fragments. "But they're going to be tough to match without a suspect vehicle."

"I'm thinking we should drive out to Metwater's camp and look for a black truck with a brush guard on the front," Dylan said.

"We will," Simon said. "But before we do, I have something else to show you."

Dylan fell into step with him as they crossed the parking lot toward Ranger Brigade headquarters. Graham met them at the door. "I was finally able to pry some more information from the FBI about Special Agent Asher and what he might have been doing here," he said.

"I thought he took personal time to come here," Dylan said.

"He did, but apparently before that he was looking into David Metwater's mob connections," Graham said.

"The twin brother, right?" Simon said.

"Right. Maybe the picture in Asher's car wasn't of Daniel Metwater, but of David."

"So you think Asher came here to talk to Metwater about his dead brother?" Dylan asked.

"Or his investigation of David turned up some dirt on Daniel." Simon strode across the room and snatched a folder off the corner of his desk. "I've been digging into the files on Asher's laptop," he said. "Pulling off as much as I can before the Feds take it away."

"Anything that will help us?" Dylan asked.

Simon flipped through the papers in the file folder. "Mostly they're notes about the Metwater brothers—everything from bank account information to some surveillance footage of either Daniel or David. I haven't figured out what it all means yet, but I will."

"So Asher may have been coming to the camp to talk to Daniel about his brother, or because he had learned something about Daniel himself, or was just generally snooping around," Dylan said. "Or he wanted to see Andi. He told her when he saw her in town that he had to talk to her."

"Maybe Asher wanted to warn her about Metwater," Graham said. "Maybe he thought she was in danger."

"Turned out Asher was the one in danger." Simon closed the folder. "Metwater may have decided to shut him up."

"Where do the two guys who attacked Kayla outside Asher's hotel room come in?" Dylan asked.

"We don't know," Graham said. "The guy who lived—Bob Casetti—is still in the hospital. He's apparently lawyered up and not talking."

Simon grunted. "When do we get to talk to him?"

"As soon as his doctor gives the okay. Meanwhile, Montrose PD is keeping a guard on his room."

"Does this Casetti have a record?" Dylan asked.

"He's been in and out of prison since he was eighteen, with sealed juvenile records before that. But mostly property crimes and drugs. No kidnapping or rape or even assault. This definitely breaks the pattern for him."

"So we ought to be able to put some pressure on him and make him talk," Simon said.

"Do you think the attack on me and Kayla last night was connected to Casetti and his dead pal kidnapping Kayla at the hotel?" Dylan asked. Getting roughed up twice in two days was too much for coincidence. "Maybe it wasn't me who was the target last night at all, but Kayla."

"It's possible," Graham said.

"Then it's not safe for her to be alone." Pushing back the icy fear that threatened to overtake him,

Dylan pulled his phone from his pocket. "I'll call and tell her I'm on my way to pick her up. We've got a vehicle I can borrow, right?"

Graham put a steadying hand on Dylan's arm. "I'll send Carmen to get her and bring her here. She can give us a statement about what happened last night, and you can take over evening guard duty if you want. But right now I want you and Simon out at the camp looking for the truck that ran you off the road."

"They've probably ditched it in the desert by now," Simon said.

"Maybe, but maybe not." Graham squeezed Dylan's shoulder, then released him. "Keep digging. If we can find a motive for Metwater to want Asher dead, we can bring him in for questioning. And let's take a closer look at Andi Matheson, too. Maybe she did meet with Asher and the conversation didn't go well."

"Did you know that Frank Asher was married?" Dylan asked.

"Why is that important?" Simon asked. "The FBI is taking care of notifying his next of kin."

"It's important because, apparently, Asher is the father of Andi Matheson's unborn child," Dylan said. "When Andi found out he was married, she broke off the relationship."

"So she might have been angry enough to shoot him when he came around to see her," Graham said.

"Maybe," Dylan said. "Though we have a lot of witnesses who place her in the camp at the time he was probably shot. And she seemed genuinely shocked when she found out he had been killed."

"We should take a closer look at her alibi," Graham said.

"We will," Dylan agreed. "But I want to question Asher's widow, too. I'd like to drive over to Denver tomorrow and find out if she—or someone she might have hired—decided to take a trip to the park about the time her late husband was killed."

"Do it." Graham shook his head. "Usually with a murder you have trouble coming up with one likely suspect. Frank Asher had any number of people who might have good reasons for wanting him dead."

"ARE YOU AS sick as I am of making the drive out here?" Simon asked as he steered his Cruiser onto the rough BLM two-track.

"Yeah." Dylan slumped in his seat and tugged the brim of his hat lower to block the midday sun glaring off the rocks that lined the road. "And I hate being out of phone range if anything happens." Before leaving Ranger headquarters, he'd called Kayla to tell her to stay put, but she had cut off his explanation, telling him she didn't have time to talk, as she was just arriving at the Montrose Police Station. Rather than argue with her, he'd called a buddy at the PD and asked them to keep Kayla there until Carmen could show up to escort her to Ranger Headquarters.

"The captain mentioned something about you and that detective driving out here last night," Simon said as they jounced along the road. "What was she doing with you?"

"Andi had asked to see Kayla yesterday afternoon, and I went with her to tell Andi that her father was missing. When Metwater discovered us, he invited us to the induction ceremony later that night."

"Why involve a civilian?" Simon asked.

"Andi knows Kayla and they seem to have established a rapport. And she knows how to handle herself. She doesn't interfere."

"She's still a civilian."

"A civilian who is helping with our investigation."

"That's one way to look at it, I guess."

They passed the rest of the drive in silence. Dylan stared out the window of the Cruiser, nursing his anger and annoyance, not to mention a headache from where he had hit his head in the crash last night. By the time Simon parked outside the camp, Dylan was more than ready to lash out at someone for all the trouble he'd been through.

"What do you think? Look around, or talk to Metwater first?" Simon asked.

"Look around." Dylan led the way down the trail into the canyon. Kiram wasn't on guard duty today. The skinny youth who was took one look at the two grim-faced officers and melted back into the rocks.

"He probably went to tell Metwater we're here," Simon said.

"Saves us the trouble," Dylan said.

The camp was quiet, the heat shimmering off the

rocks oppressive. The few people Dylan spotted were lying in hammocks in the shade or lounging in tents or makeshift brush-covered shelters. The two officers walked the length of the camp to the narrowest part of the canyon, where a few rattier tents and a lean-to made of old wooden produce crates were crowded among a collection of dilapidated cars and trucks. The intense sun had faded most of the paper labels on the flattened crates, but Dylan could still make out images of plump red tomatoes and green peppers.

A clank of metal on metal drew them around a tarp-covered shed to where two men dressed only in dirty khaki shorts leaned under the open hood of a black pickup truck with a heavy brush guard attached to the front bumper.

"Something wrong with the truck?" Dylan asked.

Zach Crenshaw jerked his head up, eyes wide, mouth open. Across from him, Abe Phillips held up the wrench. "What do you want with us, man?" he asked, his voice a nasal whine that set Dylan's teeth on edge.

"I want to know why you tried to run me down last night." Dylan took a step closer, backing the young man up against the truck and blocking his escape.

"We don't know what you're talking about." Zach had shut his mouth and regained some of his color. He motioned to the truck. "We were just trying to get this old thing running again."

"It was running fine last night when it forced my Cruiser off the road," Dylan said.

"This truck hasn't moved from this spot in a month!" Abe declared. "It doesn't even run. See for yourself." He beckoned them closer and Dylan looked under the hood at a tangle of wires and hoses, and what looked like handfuls of straw and other debris. "A pack rat built a nest in here." Abe pulled out a wad of dried grass. "Ate the wiring harness and made a mess. I haven't had a chance to get it fixed."

"Is that so?" Simon pulled out a multitool and began scraping at the brush guard, a welded pipe cage around the front grill that seemed to have more rust than paint.

"Hey, what are you doing?" Zach asked.

"I'm collecting a sample of this paint to match with the chips we took from Lieutenant Holt's Cruiser after someone ran him off the road night before last."

"It wasn't me," Abe said. "I told you, this truck hasn't moved."

"Then you don't have anything to worry about." Simon slipped the paint chips into an evidence bag and sealed it, while Dylan walked around the vehicle and took photographs from every angle.

"Why do you people always want to hassle us?" Zach asked. "We aren't doing anything but trying to live in peace."

"I wouldn't say you're doing a very good job of that so far," Dylan said. He stowed the camera. "Did

Metwater put you up to going after us last night, or was that your own idea?"

Zach swore and turned away. Abe flushed. "I told you, it wasn't us," he said. "The truck's been out of commission for weeks. I'm trying to get it running again so I can go into town."

"And do what?" Dylan asked.

"I don't know. Buy a burger and a beer. See a movie." He looked around. "Anything's better than being stuck here in the desert all the time."

"I thought this place was the Family's version of paradise," Dylan said. He kicked the front tire of the truck. "Funny that there's what looks like fresh mud and gravel in the treads of these tires, if it's just been sitting here for weeks." He sent Abe a warning look, then turned away.

"Where are you going?" Zach asked.

"To talk to Metwater."

"Don't worry, we'll be back," Simon said.

The two officers made their way toward Metwater's trailer. "So, is that the truck?" Simon asked.

"It fits the profile," Dylan said. "Though the engine did look pretty shot."

"Anyone could yank out a bunch of wires and throw in some grass and trash," Simon said.

"Even a paint match isn't going to prove anything," Dylan said. "Not if they stick to their story."

"They'll cave," Simon said. "Pointing out that fresh gravel was a nice touch. We'll lean on them some more after we talk to Metwater and we'll be hauling them back to headquarters before you know it."

"I'd rather have Metwater in handcuffs than his two flunkies," Dylan said.

"Get them into an interview room and maybe they'll spill something incriminating." They mounted the steps to Metwater's trailer and Simon knocked. No answer. He knocked again. "Metwater, this is the police. Open up!"

Silence. And no sound of movement within. Dylan moved to the tent next door. "Andi! Andi, it's Dylan Holt. Could I talk to you a minute?"

The tent flap lifted, but instead of Andi, Starfall stood in the opening. "Andi isn't here," she said.

"Where is she?"

"She said she was going for a walk." She scowled at them. "Why can't you leave her alone? She hasn't done anything to hurt anyone."

"Are you sure about that?" Simon asked.

Starfall only scowled harder.

"Do you know where Daniel Metwater is?" Dylan asked. "Did he go walking with Andi?"

"The Prophet left early this morning," she said. "If you want to talk to him, you'll have to wait until he gets back."

"Where did he go?" Simon asked.

"He speaks at gatherings around the country. I don't know where he went this time. It's not my business to know."

"When will he return?" Dylan asked.

"I don't know. It could be this evening or tomorrow or a week from now."

"Maybe he skipped out on you," Simon said.

Her eyes widened. "The Prophet would never desert us," she said.

Dylan could tell Simon was prepared to argue the point, but he cut in. "Do you know anything about Zach and Abe taking their truck out last night after the ceremony?"

She took a step back. "I don't know anything."

"You didn't see them?" Simon asked. "They ran Lieutenant Holt and the woman he was with off the road. Trashed a government vehicle and injured a law officer and a civilian. They could have been killed. If your Prophet thinks this is a good way to get us to leave him alone, he's not even half as smart as he looks."

"I don't know what you're talking about." Starfall let the tent flap fall closed.

Simon reached for it, but Dylan stayed his hand. "That's enough. We've given everyone here a lot to think about. We'll come back later when we can talk to Metwater."

"What about the truck?" Simon asked as they retraced their steps to the car.

"You heard them—it hasn't run in months."

"They might take off in it and try to run."

"They won't get far."

Simon unlocked the Cruiser and they climbed in.

"Do you think Metwater was feeling the heat and skipped town? Maybe with Andi Matheson?"

Dylan fastened his seat belt. "Anything's possible, but I don't think so. Maybe it's like she said—he's off speaking somewhere. That's one of the ways he recruits followers."

"I read some of his blog and the stuff on his website." Simon started the engine. "All about family and peace and harmony. I guess that appeals to some people."

Dylan almost laughed. "But not you?"

Simon scowled. "I live in the real world. I don't need a fantasy like that."

"Careful, Simon. You might be turning into a stereotype of a jaded cop."

"Bite me, Holt."

"I'll pass." He settled back in the seat. "We'll check in with Andi and Metwater tomorrow. If they're not around then, we can start a search. Until then, I think all we can do is wait."

Chapter Thirteen

When Kayla emerged from the Montrose Police Station after giving her statement about the previous night's hit-and-run, she was surprised to find a Ranger Brigade Cruiser snugged in beside her Subaru. Her heart beat a little faster and she quickened her pace, faltering when Carmen Redhorse emerged from the driver's seat. Then her elation edged toward panic. "What are you doing here?" she asked. "Is Dylan okay?"

"Dylan's fine." Carmen's smile was warm. "I'm here to give you a ride to Ranger headquarters so you can give us your statement. I know all this paperwork is a pain, but it's important in helping us build a case."

"I can drive myself." She started toward her car, but Carmen stepped in front of her.

"You can, but this is easier. We can swing by your place and you can drop off your car. How are you feeling? That's a nasty bruise on your face."

Kayla touched the bruise she had received two

days before in her struggle with the kidnappers. It was only a little tender now. "I'm okay. What is this really about? Did Dylan send you here?" And if he had, why?

"I take my orders from Captain Ellison, not the lieutenant. Considering you've been attacked twice in the past two days, he thought it would be a good idea to keep an eye on you."

"Why?"

Carmen wasn't smiling anymore—she looked pained. "I don't want to frighten you, but you might be in danger."

Kayla wanted to scoff at the idea, but the full meaning of Carmen's words was beginning to sink in. "Wait a minute. Do you—or the captain—think *I* was the target last night? I thought whoever hit us was going after the Cruiser. Did you find the driver? Did he tell you he was after me?"

"We don't know anything yet. We're just being careful."

"I can be careful at home." She started for her car again and this time Carmen let her open the door and slide into the driver's seat.

But when she tried to shut the door, the other woman put a hand out to stop her. "We need you to make a statement, anyway, so you might as well hang out with me for a few hours," she said.

"And then what?" Kayla asked.

The smile returned. "And then I think the captain is assigning Dylan to the night shift."

The words sent a tickle of pleasure up her spine. "I get the idea I don't really have a choice in the matter."

"We're not forcing you, but everyone would feel better if you'd come with us."

Kayla blew out a breath. If she did go home, she'd only sit there and stew. At least at Ranger headquarters she might find out more about what was going on. "All right. You can follow me to my place."

She left her car in the driveway, then joined Carmen in her Cruiser. "I really don't need a bodyguard," she said as she slid into the passenger seat.

Carmen shifted into gear and backed into the street. "Hey, I'm a tough cop and even I think it would be nice sometime to have a good-looking man worried about me," she said.

"You don't have a boyfriend?" Kayla asked, then immediately wished she could take the words back. She hated when people asked her that kind of question. "Sorry, none of my business."

"That's okay. It's a natural question. Let's just say the badge gets in the way of relationships for a lot of men. And even though I'm around men all day, it's not a good idea to get involved with anyone on the job. So that leaves, what—suspects? A few witnesses?" She shook her head. "I'm young. Someone will come along."

"I like being single," Kayla said. "I like making my own decisions and looking after myself."

"Oh, I agree," Carmen said. "It's lonely sometimes, though."

Yes, it was lonely sometimes. She hadn't often felt that way, but since she had let Dylan into her life, his absence left a space she hadn't noticed being empty before.

Ranger Brigade headquarters was a bustle of activity, though Dylan was nowhere in sight. Carmen led Kayla to her desk, where she coached her through her statement about the previous day's activities, beginning with that morning's encounters with Andi Matheson and Daniel Metwater, up to the moment of the crash. "I don't know how much good any of that will be for you," Kayla said when they were done. "I only had an impression of a fairly large vehicle, and that the driver didn't slow down, but hit us deliberately, then sped away."

"It's all part of the record," Carmen said. "Another piece in the puzzle."

The door opened and Simon entered, followed by Dylan. He spotted her right away and nodded, before turning to address Captain Ellison. "We found the truck," he said. "Can we get a warrant to impound it?"

"We can try," Ellison said. "Where is it?"

"At the camp. The two guys who were with it, Abelard Phillips and Zach Crenshaw, say it hasn't run in weeks, but I found fresh mud in the tire treads, and the color and profile fit what we're looking for. Simon got some paint samples."

"I'll get started on the warrant request," Simon said, and headed for his desk.

Dylan joined the two women. "How are you doing?" he asked Kayla. He brushed the tips of his fingers lightly over her bruised cheek.

"I'm fine." She tried to ignore the tremor of awareness his touch sent through her. "I don't need babysitting."

"Maybe not. But it will make me feel better."

She was trying to come up with a snappy retort when the door to headquarters burst open and two young men in dirty shorts and T-shirts, their faces sunburned, their hair windblown, burst in. "We want to confess," the taller of the two said. "And then we need your help."

ZACH AND ABE looked more pitiful than dangerous as Dylan and Ethan patted them down and led them to separate desks to give their statements. Dylan ended up with Abe, who limped to the chair Dylan offered and dropped into it with a groan. "We had to walk most of the way from camp before somebody gave us a ride," he said. "I think my blisters have blisters."

"Why didn't you drive your truck?" Dylan asked, taking his own seat behind the desk.

"That's why we need your help," Abe said. "The

Prophet stole it. He can't do that, right? It's my truck.
My name's on the title and everything, but he says it
belongs to the Family now—along with everything
else we brought with us, except what we could carry
out with us."

"You talked to Daniel Metwater?" Dylan asked.
"I thought he was out of town."

"He came back right after you left. Him and Asteria. I guess they only went up to Grand Junction or
something. Anyway, Starfall must have blabbed that
you were there and why, and he kicked us out. Told us
to get whatever we could carry—but nothing else—
and hit the road." He leaned toward Dylan. "That's
stealing, right? We can file charges, can't we?"

"Why don't we start at the beginning," Dylan said.
"You said you wanted to confess to something?"

Abe sank back in his chair. "Yeah, that." He
glanced around nervously. "Promise you're not going
to beat me up or anything?"

"Just tell me what happened." Dylan had no in-
tention of hurting the kid, but a little fear might persuade him to be more cooperative.

"After you interrupted the ceremony last night we
were really ticked off that you kept hassling everybody. We're just out here trying to live in peace and
you keep poking your nose where it doesn't belong."

"So you decided to teach us a lesson."

"Well…" He looked away.

"Did Daniel Metwater know what you intended?"

"We told him someone needed to do something, and he agreed."

"Did he tell you to follow us?"

"No. But we thought he approved. We thought it would be a good way to impress him." Abe looked glum. "I guess we should have known better."

"What happened?"

"Zach and I got in my truck and followed you out onto the highway. Then we rammed you and sent you into the ditch. We just wanted to shake you up and make you think twice about hassling us. We didn't mean to hurt anyone or anything."

"Why did you shoot at us?"

Abe flushed. "I was trying to shoot out the tires, but I guess I'm not a very good shot."

"You told me before that you didn't have a gun. That the Prophet didn't allow it."

"Yeah, well, last time we went into town I bought one, anyway. He's got a gun, and I was tired of eating so much tofu and vegetables. Not when the place is crawling with rabbits."

"Where is the gun now?"

"The Prophet made me hand it over to him. I mean, we were trying to help him and he raked us over the coals."

"You said he kicked you out?"

"Yeah. He said we were troublemakers. First with that guy who died, then this."

"What about the guy who died? Why did Metwater blame you for what happened to him?"

"Not for what happened to him, but for bringing him into camp. He said it caused bad juju and that was the reason the cops were around all the time. But we couldn't have just left him in the desert for the buzzards. That's just cold."

"What was Metwater doing this afternoon, while he was away from the camp?" Dylan asked.

"I don't know. Only those in his inner circle—his favorites—ever know what he's up to." Abe gave a snorting laugh. "We don't have the right chromosomes for that, if you know what I mean."

"You're not women."

"Right. He needs guys around for security and heavy lifting, but it's really the chicks he likes. We thought when we joined up we'd have access to all these hot women, but the Prophet keeps them all for himself."

"You say he was with Andi Matheson this afternoon?"

"Who?"

"Asteria."

"Oh, yeah. They were all cozy and laughing. She's definitely one of the inner circle. So can you help us get our stuff back? I mean, he can't just take it, can he?"

Dylan gave him a hard look. "You're confessing

to attacking a law enforcement officer and you expect us to help you get your stuff back?"

He squirmed. "Well, yeah. We're pleading guilty in exchange for a deal."

"What kind of deal?"

He leaned forward again and lowered his voice. "We know a lot of dirt on the Prophet. We tell you what we know in exchange for…what do you call it—like a flu shot?"

"Immunity?"

"Right, immunity."

"What do you know about the Prophet?"

"Good stuff, I promise. The guy might look snowy white outside, but he's definitely not."

"You're going to have to be more specific than that if you want to avoid going to jail."

Abe went pale under his sunburn at the word *jail*. "Well, like, everybody who joins the Family has to sign a contract that says all the property you have belongs to the group, but what it really means is that it belongs to the Prophet. But that can't be legal, right?"

"If you signed the contract willingly, it might."

"People only sign it because he promises all this stuff—eternal riches and joy and peace, things like that. And then you end up living in the middle of nowhere on tofu, sleeping in tents, and the hot girls won't even give you the time of day."

"I'm going to need more than that if I'm going

to persuade the district attorney to cut you a deal," Dylan said.

"Aww, man! We don't have to get attorneys involved, do we?"

Dylan remained silent, arms crossed over his chest.

Abe sighed. "All right. How about this? His name isn't even Daniel Metwater."

"No?" Dylan raised one eyebrow.

"No. I was in his RV one time and I saw a bunch of papers and his driver's license, in a folder on his desk. They all said *David* Metwater. Not Daniel, see? Maybe if you run that name through your computers, you'll find out he has a criminal record or something."

"He had a twin brother named David. The brother died. It wouldn't be that unusual for him to have kept his brother's papers."

Abe looked crestfallen.

"Where was Metwater the morning you and Zach found that man's body?" Dylan asked.

"He was in the camp."

"You saw him?"

"Yeah. Right before we went hunting. He was eating breakfast with Asteria and Starfall and a bunch of others."

"What was he doing before that?"

Zach scowled. "We all had to get up early for this sunrise ceremony. He's big into that kind of thing.

I mean, the middle of the night, practically, he expects us all to get up and dance around and chant, and then he delivers a 'message.' After a while it's just the same stuff over and over."

"Sounds like you were getting pretty disillusioned by the whole experience," Dylan said.

"Well, yeah. I mean, I like some of his ideas, and I really don't mind the camping out and stuff, but I thought it would be more fun. And that there would be more women—or at least women who would give me the time of day."

Dylan slid back his chair and rose. "I'll see what I can do, Abe, but I'm not making any promises."

He left to confer with Graham, but on his way he stopped by Carmen's desk to speak with Kayla. "Anything interesting?" she asked, nodding toward Abe.

"I think he found out being part of Metwater's 'family' isn't the laid-back paradise he was picturing when he signed up. He gives Metwater a solid alibi for the morning Asher was killed, though. Apparently he was in plain sight of most of the Family members from sunrise on." Dylan leaned over, one hand on the back of her chair. "I need to stay and interview him and Zach some more, and talk with some other people. I'll find someone to take you home and stay with you at your place."

"I don't need anyone to stay with me," she said. "I mean, you have the guys who hit us in custody now."

"They weren't specifically after you, anyway," he said. "Just dumb and ticked off, trying to scare us a little."

"They succeeded there." She stood and he walked with her to the door. "Do you think they'll give you any useful information?"

"I don't know. But we have to try." He squeezed her shoulder. "You're sure you'll be okay alone?"

"I can look after myself. I've been doing it a long time."

"I'll probably be here late, and in the morning I have to go to Denver. It may be a while before I see you again."

A hint of a smile touched the corners of her mouth. "I can wait."

Maybe she only meant the words politely, but he took them as a promise of more. A promise he intended to collect on when he returned.

Chapter Fourteen

Midnight had come and gone by the time Dylan and the other Rangers sent Abe and Zach to cool their heels overnight in the Montrose County Jail. Ethan and Simon were going to continue the interviews the next morning in hopes of getting something more useful out of them, but beyond a hint at some questionable financial practices, the two had so far produced no evidence of a serious crime.

Dylan sent Kayla a text before he left town. Have a good day and be careful, he typed.

You, too.

As romantic words went, they weren't much, but she wasn't resisting him the way she once had, so he took that as a good sign. He checked out a new Cruiser from the Ranger Brigade fleet and made the drive to Denver in a good mood despite a short night's sleep, and a little after noon he found the house in the Denver suburb of Highlands Ranch the Ashers called home.

Veronica Asher was a tall, curvy woman with dark skin who wore her black hair in dozens of long braids that hung past her shoulder blades. She answered the door of the stone-and-cedar home with a toddler on one hip and two other children peeking from around her legs. "Yes?" She eyed Dylan skeptically.

"Mrs. Asher? Dylan Holt, Colorado State Patrol." He held up his credentials. "I'm sorry to bother you, but I'm investigating your husband's death and I need to ask you some questions."

She held the door open wider, then shifted the baby. "Frankie, you take your sisters to the kitchen and tell MeMaw I said you could have ice cream."

"Okay, Mama." The boy eyed Dylan warily, but took the baby from his mother and left the room.

Mrs. Asher watched them go, then turned back to Dylan. "The FBI has already been to see me," she said.

"They may be conducting their own investigation, but I'm part of a task force charged with dealing with crimes on public land. Since your husband was killed in the Curecanti Wilderness Area, a federal preserve, we're looking into his murder."

She sat on the sofa and smoothed her skirt across her knees. Her beautiful face bore the marks of grief in her haunted eyes and drawn expression. "I'll tell you the same thing I told the Feds," she said. "I don't have any idea what Frank was doing out there in the middle of nowhere. He told me he had to work on a case—for his job. But the FBI tells me he was on personal leave."

"So he lied to you," Dylan said.

"It wasn't the first time."

He studied her—a beautiful, weary woman who had been betrayed by the man who had promised to love and care for her. Was that enough for her to have left those children and driven five hours across the state to murder him? "Mrs. Asher, you say you don't know what your husband was doing out there in the wilderness area, but do you have an idea? Any suspicions?"

"Maybe he went to see that girl he was sneaking around with."

"What girl?"

"I don't think you made it to lieutenant without being a better investigator than that," she said.

"What girl, Mrs. Asher?"

She looked away, her body rigid, as if it took everything in her to hold back the rage—or the tears. "Frank was having an affair with a girl young enough to be his daughter. Senator Pete Matheson's daughter, Andi."

"So you think Frank arranged to meet Andi in the wilderness area?"

"No, I think he arranged to meet her in a hotel.

That's what he usually did. I have no idea how he ended up in the desert with his head blown off. Maybe he had another side dish I didn't know about and she had a jealous husband or boyfriend who followed Frank out there and did him in." She looked at him again. "If you find out who did it, be sure and let me know so I can shake his hand."

"Mrs. Asher, where were you on August 14?"

"I was right here. I took my older children to school and my baby to the pediatrician. I had lunch with my mother and bought groceries in the afternoon, and after the children went to bed I drank half a bottle of wine and cried myself to sleep, trying to decide whether it was worth putting my children through losing their father in order to divorce my cheating husband. What I was not doing was driving halfway across the state to shoot him."

"I have to ask," Dylan said.

"I know. But while you're at it, you ought to ask Andi Matheson what she was up to on August 14."

"I've already spoken to Ms. Matheson. Why do you think she could have killed your husband?"

"Maybe he cheated on her, too. Maybe she got tired of his lies."

"Did your husband lie to you about other things—things besides other women?"

"Haven't you been paying attention? The man worked for the FBI. His whole job was telling lies—deceiving people and pretending to be someone he wasn't in order to gather information. Too bad it got to be a habit he couldn't break."

"Do you know anyone else who might have disliked Frank enough to murder him?" Dylan asked.

"I imagine Frank made plenty of enemies, but I can't tell you who they are."

"Have you scheduled any kind of funeral service for your husband?"

"Why? Do you think all his enemies will want to come and gloat?" She looked away again. "I'm sorry. That was uncalled for. The service is Thursday. Grace Memorial Chapel, 6:00 p.m."

An older woman appeared in the archway between the living room where they sat and the hall. "It's time for Kendra's nap," she said, ignoring Dylan. "You know she always goes down better for you."

"It would be better if you left now." Veronica stood.

"If we learn any more about your husband's death, we'll pass the information along to you," Dylan said. "I'm sorry for your loss."

"Oh, yeah, we're all real sorry." She ushered him to the door. "If you find out who did this, send me a report. I don't promise to read it, but I can at least save it for the children. I'm sure they'll have questions one day. Maybe it would be good to have some answers."

Dylan sat in the Ranger Cruiser in the Ashers'

driveway and studied the neat suburban home. He couldn't understand what would compel a man like Frank to betray his family the way he had. Dylan's own father would have cut off his arm rather than hurt his wife and children. Dylan intended to live his life the same way.

He pulled out his phone and scrolled to Kayla's number. "Hi," he said when she answered. "How's your day going?"

"Okay." She sounded suspicious as always. He wanted to remind her that she could trust him, but trust wasn't something you could persuade people to do with words. Kayla would have to learn to trust him in her own time. "Are you in Denver?" she asked.

"Yes. I just talked to Frank Asher's widow."

"And?"

He glanced toward the house and thought he saw a curtain twitch. Mrs. Asher and her mother were probably wondering when he was going to leave. "I don't think she killed her husband," he said. "We'll check her alibi, but I'm betting it holds."

"Which leaves who—one of Daniel Metwater's disciples?"

"Or Andi Matheson."

"I'm not buying it," Kayla said. "You know it could be some other person we haven't even zeroed in on yet."

"It could be. But what were they doing out in the desert that morning, so near Metwater's camp?"

"I guess if you can figure that out, you'll know who did it."

"There's a memorial service for Frank Asher Thursday. Want to come with me and see if anyone interesting shows up?"

"Is this your idea of a hot date?"

Was she flirting with him? That was a good sign, wasn't it? "If you agree to come with me, I'm sure I could make it worth your while."

"Are you expecting Frank's killer?" she said. "I think criminals watch enough TV these days not to fall for that trap."

"You never can tell. Do you want to come?"

"Sorry, I can't."

"What if I throw in dinner and a movie after the services?"

"You're really tempting me, but I have somewhere else I have to be."

"Somewhere more important than the funeral of a man you didn't know?"

She laughed. "It's just a meeting of the Western Slope private investigators, but I have to go."

"They can't have the meeting without you? Are you on the board? The guest speaker?"

"You're going to make me tell you, aren't you?"

"I'm very persistent."

She sighed. "I'm getting an award."

"Congratulations. What award?"

"It's stupid. Western Slope Private Investigator of the Year. I'm sure it will just be some cheesy certificate or something."

"It sounds like a big deal to me. I can't believe you didn't want to tell me."

"Honestly, I don't even want to go. I'd rather attend Frank's funeral. But I don't think I can get out of it without causing a fuss."

"Go. Get your honor and celebrate. Congratulations."

"Think of me while you're at Frank's service," she said. "And let me know if anyone mysterious shows up."

He ended the call and left the Asher house. He couldn't believe Kayla had won this honor and hadn't even told him. She probably hadn't told anyone. She acted almost embarrassed at the thought of anyone making a fuss over her. Maybe her family hadn't been one to celebrate accomplishments the way his had. His mom had even baked a cake to celebrate Dylan's first touchdown on the high school football team.

His phone rang and he punched the button on the steering wheel to answer it. "Dylan, it's Carmen." The voice of his fellow Ranger sounded clear over the speaker. "Did you get anything from Frank Asher's widow?"

"We'll need to check her alibi, but it sounds like

she was busy here all day with the family. As much as she feels betrayed by Frank, I don't think she would have killed her children's father."

"Are you on your way back to Montrose?"

"I am."

"Good. We've had a new development. Andi Matheson showed up here a few minutes ago. She's pretty distraught. She says her father's dead."

"LARIMER INVESTIGATIONS. How may I help you?"

"This is Simon Woolridge with the Ranger Brigade."

The familiar clipped voice set Kayla's heart to pounding. She gripped the phone more tightly. "Is something wrong?" she asked.

"Andi Matheson is here at Ranger headquarters and she's asking for you. I tried to tell her you're a private detective, not law enforcement, but she's emotional. Can you get over here and see if you can calm her down?"

"I'm on my way." She shut down her computer and gathered her purse and car keys. Andi must be really upset if Snooty Simon had resorted to calling her. Had something happened at the camp? Or to her baby?

When she arrived at Ranger Brigade headquarters, she found Simon and a handsome BLM agent, who introduced himself as Michael Dance, clustered around a wailing Andi Matheson, who sat slumped in a chair. "Kayla!" she screamed when she saw her enter the room.

Kayla rushed to the young woman and bent to wrap her arms around her. "Andi, what's wrong?"

Michael brought Kayla a chair and she slid into it. Andi clung to her, her whole body shaking with sobs. "She's been this way for the last half hour," Michael said softly. "Ever since she got here."

"Andi, honey, calm down." Kayla pushed damp hair away from the young woman's tear-swollen eyes. "It's not good for the baby for you to be so upset. Tell me what's wrong and I'll do everything I can to help you."

"It's Daddy. He's dead!"

Kayla looked at Simon. He shook his head. "We don't know any more than you do," he said.

"Daddy's dead!" Andi wailed.

"Andi, look at me." Kayla grasped the woman's chin and turned it toward her. "How do you know your father is dead? Have you seen him?"

"Daniel told me he's dead. Daniel would never lie to me." A fresh wave of sobs engulfed her.

"Somebody get her some water, please," Kayla said.

Simon filled a paper cup at the watercooler by the door and brought it to her. "Drink this," Kayla ordered, and held it to the young woman's lips.

Andi obediently took a sip. "I can't stand it," she whispered. "I always thought I'd have time to see him again. I said such awful things the last time we were together." She rested her head on Kayla's shoulder and sobbed.

Kayla shook her gently. "Pull yourself together, Andi. Tell me exactly what Daniel said to you that has you so upset."

Andi sniffed and sat up a little straighter, wiping at her eyes with the back of her hand.

"Here, ma'am." Simon handed her several tissues from a box that sat near the cooler.

"Thank you." Andi blew her nose, then took a deep breath and turned to Kayla. "Daniel called me into his RV this afternoon and told me he had some sad news for me, but that I needed to be strong for the baby's sake."

"You are strong, Andi." Kayla squeezed her arm. "Strong enough to tell me everything that happened." She noticed Simon had grabbed a notebook from a nearby desk and was prepared to write everything down. "What did Daniel say?"

"He told me my father was dead. That I shouldn't be sad because he was in a better place now."

"Did Metwater say how he knew this?" Simon asked.

Kayla glared at him, but Andi didn't seem to notice. "He said he saw Daddy's body in a dream," she said, her voice choked with tears. "He said there was blood all over him, and that he knew that meant he was dead."

"Think very carefully," Kayla said. "This is really important. Did Daniel say he saw your father in a dream, or just that he saw your father?"

"He said he saw him in a dream." She looked at Kayla, her blue eyes as wide and innocent as a child's. "He's a prophet. He knows these things. If he saw Daddy dead, it must be true."

Kayla held her close, trying to comfort her. Someone needed to strangle Daniel Metwater and tell him to keep his phony prophecies to himself. What had he hoped to accomplish by upsetting Andi this way?

At last Andi's sobs subsided. She sat up and pushed her hair out of her eyes. "I have to get back to camp," she said. "It's almost time for dinner and I have to help cook." She squeezed Kayla's hand. "I just wanted someone else to know. A friend."

Kayla's eyes stung, she was so touched by these words. "I'm glad you came to me," she said.

"We'll drive you back," Simon said. "And while we're there we can have a word with Daniel."

"How did you get here?" Kayla asked.

"I hiked to the road and hitched a ride with a tourist," Andi said. She stood and Kayla rose also.

"I'll ride with you to the camp," Kayla said.

"That won't be necessary," Simon said.

"Please let Kayla come with me." Andi grabbed her hand and squeezed so hard she winced.

Simon scowled at her, then turned away. "Come on, then."

Chapter Fifteen

Andi remained subdued on the ride back to the camp. She stared out the window in the backseat of Simon's Cruiser. Kayla thought she might even have fallen asleep for a little while.

Up front, Simon and Michael didn't speak, either. Kayla knew Simon resented her presence, but she didn't care. Andi wanted her company, so she would do what she could to comfort her. Besides, she wasn't going to miss the chance to see what Daniel Metwater had to say for himself. Had he really seen Peter Matheson in a dream, or did he know the senator was dead because he'd killed him?

They arrived at the parking area for the camp and Andi opened her door before the Cruiser had come to a full stop. "Thanks for the ride," she said. "I have to hurry and help with dinner."

Simon reached to pull her back, but Kayla grabbed his arm. "Let her go," she said. "You'll have better luck with Metwater without her there, getting worked up again."

He pulled his arm away. "Don't tell me how to do my job."

"She's right," Michael said. "Metwater might be more candid without one of his pretty followers to impress."

Simon said nothing, but turned and led the way up the path to the camp, Michael and Kayla walking single file behind him. The camp seemed busier than usual, with at least a dozen people moving about among the collection of tents and trailers. An older woman supervised two men who were unloading supplies from a battered blue Volkswagen bus. A trio of children played with a black dog, throwing a stick and laughing as he retrieved it. Other women milled around the cooking fire in the center of the camp, while a group of men and women worked to construct a kind of brush arbor in front of one of the trailers.

Several of the campers stopped to stare as the trio made their way across the compound, the utility belts of the two officers rattling with each step. They climbed the steps to Metwater's RV and Simon knocked.

No answer. Simon pounded harder. "Maybe he's not in," Kayla said.

Simon looked around. "Where's Metwater?" he called to a passing woman.

She stared at him, then shook her head and fled.

Simon beat on the door again. "Metwater, if you don't open up in three I'm going to break the door down."

"Can he do that?" Kayla whispered to Michael.

"He's concerned for the occupant's welfare," Michael said, stone-faced.

"One. Two."

The door opened and Daniel Metwater, in jeans and a loose shirt, glared at them. "You have no right to intrude on my home," he said.

Simon shouldered past him and the others followed. "If you prefer we can take you back to headquarters for questioning," Simon said. "Your choice." He turned to the young woman who sat on the black leather sectional that filled most of the RV's living room. "You can leave now, miss."

She hurried away, not even pausing to say goodbye to Metwater. After the door had closed behind her, Simon addressed Metwater again. "Do you want to come with us, or answer our questions here?"

"I don't have anything to say to you." He flopped onto the couch, one arm stretched along the back, the casualness of the pose a sharp contrast to Simon's rigid posture.

Kayla sat on the other end of the sectional. Metwater's eyes followed her, but he said nothing. "Andi came to see me and she was very upset by some things you had told her," she said.

"There was no need for that," Metwater said. "She

would have found all the comfort she needed here, with her brothers and sisters."

"She said you told her her father, Senator Matheson, was dead." Simon, still standing, moved between Kayla and Metwater. "How did you know that?"

"I have prophetic dreams," Metwater said. "I don't expect you to understand."

"Then you must have known as soon as we heard about this particular prophecy we'd be here to question you," Simon said.

"Prophecy doesn't work that way. I only receive the messages my higher power wants me to have."

"So your higher power told you the senator was dead."

Simon's snide tone probably wasn't helping the situation any, but Kayla kept quiet, shifting to the right so she could watch Daniel as he spoke. "I saw Senator Matheson's body in a dream," he said. "He was covered in blood. Too much blood to be alive."

"Or maybe you saw his body in real life," Simon said. "When you killed him."

"I didn't kill the senator." Metwater's expression remained indifferent. "I've never even met him."

"How did he die?" Michael, who had remained standing near the door, spoke for the first time.

"I don't know," Metwater said.

"Where is he now?" Michael asked.

"I don't know that, either. All I saw was his body in a dream."

"And that was enough for you to decide to upset Ms. Matheson by telling her her father was dead?" Simon demanded. Kayla thought she detected real anger in his expression.

"What is upsetting for her now will be better for her in the long run."

"And who are you to decide that?" Simon loomed over him. "The poor woman was devastated. Did you enjoy that? Did you enjoy deliberately causing her pain?"

Metwater straightened. "Now she can grieve and get on with her life. She can finally cut her last ties with her old life and move into a brighter future."

"Was that your plan all along?" Simon asked. "Get rid of her lover, Frank Asher. Then get rid of her father. What about the child? Do you plan to do away with it, too?"

Metwater shoved himself to his feet, so that he was nose to nose with him. "Get out!"

"I could arrest you," Simon said.

"For what? For having a dream?"

The two men stared at each other for a long, tense moment. Kayla glanced at Michael and saw that he had moved closer, his right hand hovering over the gun at his side, ready to defend his fellow officer if Metwater attacked.

Simon took a step back. "If I find out what you

saw was more than a dream, I'll be back," he said. He strode out of the RV and the others followed.

"Kayla." Metwater stopped her at the door.

Startled, she turned. "Yes?"

"Is Asteria—Andi—going to be all right?" he asked. "I thought knowing her father was at peace would be better than the uncertainty of not knowing what had happened to him. Then she left here, so upset, and I heard she had left the camp altogether. I sent people after her, but they couldn't find her. I didn't think she would go to the Rangers."

His concern seemed genuine. "Have you ever lost someone you were close to?" Kayla asked.

His expression darkened. "My father and I were not close. I was always a disappointment to him."

"What about your brother? Didn't I read he died last year?"

"Yes." He looked away. "Yes, David and I were close."

"Then you know a little of what Andi is going through right now. If her father really is dead—and she can't be sure until the body is found—it will take her time to process what has happened and heal. You can help by letting her take things at her own pace. Be there for her, but don't press her to behave any certain way."

"I'll keep that in mind. And thank you—for being a friend to Asteria, and for not judging me so harshly."

Simon and Michael were waiting at the bottom of the steps when Kayla emerged from Metwater's trailer. They said nothing on the walk back to the Cruiser, but once they were all buckled in, Simon turned to her. "What did Metwater have to say to you after we left?" he asked.

"He wanted to know if I thought Andi would be all right."

Simon grunted and started the car. The ride back to Ranger headquarters was as silent as the journey there had been, until they turned onto the highway. "What's your impression of Metwater?" Simon asked.

Kayla looked up and met his eyes in the rearview mirror. "I'm surprised my opinion matters to you," she said.

"Dylan said you were a good observer, and a good judge of character."

This information pleased her more than she cared to admit. She considered her impression of Metwater. "I think a man would have to be arrogant beyond belief to kill a man, then describe seeing the body and try to pass it off as a dream," she said.

"Metwater is pretty arrogant," Michael pointed out.

"Yes, but he's also very smart," she said.

"So you're saying you think he really had a dream where he saw Pete Matheson's body covered in blood?" Simon asked.

"Maybe. I mean, it doesn't sound logical, but I guess stranger things have happened." Her father liked to claim he had prophetic dreams, too—usually as a way of providing "evidence" to support whatever decision he had already made. But a few times his dreams had been eerily prescient. Kayla had always dismissed this as coincidence, but still...

"Peter Matheson is missing," she said. "When someone goes missing, death is always a possibility, so Metwater may be manipulating that possibility to make himself look good."

"How so?" Michael turned to look over the seat at her.

"He says he saw the senator dead. If we find a body, he can say he foretold it, and show how powerful he is. He impresses his current followers and makes them even more loyal, and maybe he recruits a few new ones. If the senator turns up all right, Matheson can say what he saw in his dream was the senator injured—either physically or psychically—and he merely misinterpreted the image. He'll manage to talk his followers into seeing this as another example of how tuned in he is with a higher power."

"You've given a lot of thought to this," Simon said. "I'm impressed. And I agree—Metwater is up to something. And we're going to find out what."

THE SUN WAS setting by the time Dylan pulled into Ranger Brigade headquarters, and his shoulders ached from so many hours behind the wheel. Michael Dance looked up from his desk when Dylan entered. "How was Denver?" he asked.

"It's a big city with too much traffic." He glanced around the empty office. "What happened with Andi Metwater? Did they really find the senator?"

"Pull up a chair and I'll fill you in."

A half hour later Dylan sat back and shook his head. "And Peter Matheson still hasn't turned up—dead or alive?"

"We checked and there's been no sign of him, nor any indication of foul play. The Feds checked out his house and his office. He's vanished. But Metwater sure convinced Andi that her father is dead."

"And we don't have any proof Metwater killed him."

"None." Michael drummed on his desk with a pencil. "And why admit knowledge of the crime if he did do it? He had to know it would focus all our attention on him as suspect number one."

"What about Zach and Abe? Did you get anything more out of them?"

"Not really. The district attorney agreed to a lesser charge of leaving the scene of an accident and reckless driving. They both have clean records, so they'll probably get off with a fine and probation. And they've agreed to remain available if we have any more questions."

"They're lucky to get off so lightly."

"Except they're still crying about Metwater taking their stuff. We told them that was a civil matter they needed to take up with a lawyer. After all, they did voluntarily sign everything over to the Prophet."

"I'm beginning to think that whole bunch over there are crazy," Dylan said.

"Crazy like a fox," Michael said. "Kayla thinks Metwater is using this so-called prophecy to manipulate his followers to think he has special powers. If the senator really is dead, he predicted it. If Matheson turns up safe and sound he can offer a different interpretation of his dream and still make himself look right."

Dylan nodded. "I guess it makes sense in a twisted way."

"She's pretty smart—Kayla, I mean." Michael gave him a long look.

"What?" Dylan asked.

"Are you two, you know, together?"

"I'm not sleeping with her, if that's what you're asking."

"No, that's not what I was asking. Relax. I just thought you seemed interested in her. And you've been spending a lot of time together."

Dylan shoved himself out of his chair. "Yeah, I'm interested in her. But I'm not sure she feels the same way about me."

"Has she told you to back off?"

"No."

"Then she's interested." Michael grinned.

"Who made you an expert?" Dylan asked. "They told me you were still a newlywed."

"Yep. And I met my wife while working on a case. She found a body in the wilderness, too. And she wasn't that crazy about me the first time we met, but I won her over." He stood also. "I'm calling it a night."

"Yeah, me, too." They left together, headed in the same direction out of the parking lot. But when Michael turned off toward the duplex he and his wife, Abbie, rented near the park, Dylan continued into town.

It was almost eight o'clock when he parked in front of Kayla's house. Light glowed from the front windows and he caught the scent of jasmine from the vine that wound up the porch post. Maybe it was too late to drop in. He sat in the Cruiser, debating, until the front door opened. "Do you want to come in, or are you staking out the place?" Kayla called.

He climbed out of the car and went to her. He didn't even wait for her to say anything, but pulled her close and kissed her—long and hard, not holding back how much he wanted her. She went very still at first, then melted against him, her arms around his back, letting him take what he wanted.

When at last he released her, she took a step back, her cheeks flushed. "What was that for?" she asked, searching his face.

"I had a hard day and I needed to kiss you." He walked past her into the house.

She closed the door and followed him into the kitchen, where he was leaning into the open refrigerator. "I'm starved," he said. "I could use a sandwich, and a beer."

She grabbed his arm and tugged him away from the fridge. "Sit down. I'll fix you something to eat. Tell me about your day."

"You first," he said, settling into a chair. "I want to know about Andi Matheson. I hear she showed up at the office, distraught."

"Did you also hear why? That Daniel Metwater had a dream about her father?"

"Yeah. Ethan filled me in. Is she going to be okay?"

"I think so." Kayla took a bottle of beer from the refrigerator, opened it and handed it to him. "In a way, her faith in Metwater, or in whatever he represents for her, will help her in her grief, though I wanted to shake him for being an idiot."

Dylan took a long pull of the beer and felt more of the day's tension drain away. "Ethan said you thought Metwater cooked the whole thing up to make himself look good," he said.

"Probably." She pulled out bread, meat and cheese and began assembling a sandwich.

He watched her work, smooth and competent, her brow creased in thought. "Did your father do that

kind of thing?" he asked. "Make predictions to manipulate people?"

"Oh, yes. He was a master at it. Even I believed
him, when I was too young to know better." She
turned to face Dylan. "When I was seven, more than
anything I wanted this particular doll that was pop-
ular at the time. One of those dolls that come with
a storybook and matching outfits and furniture and
everything. My father told me that if I prayed and
had enough faith, I would get the doll for Christmas. I spent hours on my knees that November and
December. By the time Christmas came I was absolutely certain that doll would be mine."

"And you didn't get it." He could read the pain in
her eyes, a wound that lingered even after all these
years.

"No. I was heartbroken. When I started crying,
my father told me it was my own fault, because I
didn't have enough faith." She turned back to the
sandwich. "I think that was when I stopped believing at all."

Dylan's fingers tightened around his beer. What
kind of person treated a child that way? "Where was
your mother?" he asked.

"Oh, she always went along with whatever my father said. She was an obedient servant, like we were
all supposed to be. But I couldn't do it. I couldn't be
good and follow orders only on his say-so. I had to
see a reason behind his commands, and too often

there wasn't any logic, just what he had decided he wanted, or what would make the best impressions on others."

"I wish I had known you then," Dylan said. "I would have told you you were better and smarter than any of them."

She set the sandwich in front of him. "Don't fret over it. I don't. Or not usually."

"That's right," he said. "After all, you're the private investigator of the year."

"On the Western Slope of Colorado. There aren't that many of us." She took another beer from the refrigerator, opened it and sat across from him. "There are also awards for rookie of the year for a brand-new PI, awards for senior investigators and heroism on the job and who knows what else. Apparently, when the current president took over, she was determined to wring as much publicity as possible out of what had been a fairly sedate dinner."

"So have you picked out a new dress to wear, and practiced your acceptance speech?" he asked.

She rolled her eyes. "I don't even want to think about it." She sipped from her beer. "Tell me about your day. You saw Frank Asher's widow. What else?"

"That was enough." He took a bite of sandwich, chewed and swallowed. "It isn't the violence of this job that gets to me," he said. "I expected that. And the danger—well, most cops will admit that can be a rush. But what grinds me down sometimes is all the ways people can be mean to each other. I sat there with Veronica Asher and all I saw was a beautiful woman, a devoted mother and daughter, who was worn out with grief and hurt. Her husband made a promise to be there for her and then he broke it. And Andi Matheson was hurt, too—by Frank Asher's lies and by Daniel Metwater's manipulation. You were hurt by your parents, and hearing about it makes me want to do something to make it right, but I know there's nothing I can do—for any of you."

She stood and came around the table and put her hand on his shoulder. "Move your chair back."

He scooted it back and she sat in his lap. "Being with you makes me feel better," she said. "Isn't that enough?" She kissed his cheek, then his lips.

He wrapped his arms around her and pulled her closer still, her breasts soft against his chest, her mouth warm and fervent, her tongue tangling with his, tasting of ale and promising a hundred ways to make him forget pain and worry and stress.

He caressed her thigh and moved from her mouth to feather kisses along her jaw. "If you're trying to distract me, it's working."

"Don't mind me." She began to unbutton his khaki uniform shirt. "Finish your sandwich."

"What sandwich?" He slid his hand beneath her T-shirt, the flesh of her torso soft and cool beneath his fingers. He skimmed over her bra, dragging his thumb across her pebbled nipple, and smiled at the way her breath caught. She squirmed, and it was his turn to gasp as she rubbed against his growing erection. She had most of the buttons on his shirt undone now, and bent to trace her tongue along his breastbone.

He nudged his thumb beneath her chin until she raised her head and met his gaze. "Not that this isn't fun, but where are we going with it?" he asked.

"I was thinking eventually we could go into the bedroom," she said. "Though I have a nice sofa, too, if that's more your speed. I wouldn't recommend the kitchen table, though."

"The bedroom sounds good." He rose, and she slid from his lap, though he steadied her with his arm. "You lead the way."

She glanced back at the table. "Are you sure you don't want to finish your sandwich?"

"Later." He nudged her bottom.

Kayla's bedroom turned out to be down a short hall, a small, comfortable room decorated in shades of blue, with a faded flowered quilt on the bed. The air smelled like her—soft and faintly floral. Fresh. In the doorway, she drew him to her once more and undid the final button on his shirt.

He went to work on the zipper of her jeans. "This is the nicest surprise I've had all day," he said.

"Why is it a surprise?" she asked. "You must have known I was attracted to you."

"I hoped, but you weren't sending the clearest

signals. Or maybe I just wasn't good at interpreting them."

She shoved the shirt off his shoulders. "Is this a clear enough signal for you?"

"Oh, yeah." He slid out of the shirt, then pushed up the hem of hers. "Loud and clear."

He liked that she wasn't shy about undressing. And she didn't seem to mind that he waited until she was naked before he finished shedding his own clothes. She had a slim, athletic body, with small breasts and rounded hips. Her skin was so soft, and touching her sent a thrill of desire through him. He cupped her breast and she arched to him, and when he bent to take her nipple in his mouth, she let out a long sigh that pierced him.

She urged him toward the bed, paused to fold back the covers, then pulled him on top of her. When her lips found his he closed his eyes and lost himself in her embrace, forgetting time and place and everything but the feel of her body beneath his roaming hands and lips. She responded with a fervor to match his own, kissing and caressing until he was half-mad with wanting her.

"Tell me you have a condom somewhere in this house," he murmured into the side of her neck.

"Bedside table."

He shoved himself up, reached for the drawer on the little table and pulled out a gold box. "These aren't even open," he said, frowning at the plastic wrapping.

"I bought a new box just for you." She laughed and snatched the package from him. "Go back to what you were doing. I wouldn't want to slow you dow—" The last word died on her lips as he slid down the length of her body to the juncture of her thighs.

"Don't let me slow you down," he said, his attention focused on her sex.

"Don't you dare stop," she said, and he heard the plastic on the box rip.

He slid his hands up to caress her hips, and lost himself in pleasuring her. Her soft moans and breathy gasps encouraged him, as he worked to bring her close to the edge, but not over. She let out a cry of frustration when he slid back up her body to lie beside her. "There's more where that came from," he said.

"Promise?" She pushed him onto his back and climbed on top of him, then took the unwrapped condom from the bedside table. "Ready to get dressed?" she asked.

"Ready."

Kayla kept her gaze focused on Dylan's face as she rolled on the condom. She'd fantasized about being with him, but the reality was so much better. He approached lovemaking with the perfect combination of humor and seriousness that kept her from feeling awkward, and his obvious eagerness for her bolstered her confidence and fueled her own desire.

His eyes lost focus as she squeezed his shaft, and she felt a sharpened pull of desire deep within her. Maybe she had wanted a man this much before, but she didn't think so. With Dylan she felt less wary, freer to be herself, than with any other man, and that freedom was a powerful aphrodisiac. He grasped her hips and guided her over him, and she let out a long sigh as he filled her. Yes, this was definitely one of the best decisions she had made in a while.

She set the pace, rocking slowly, then sliding up and down the length of him, enjoying the sensation, drawing out the pleasure, until he thrust up more firmly and dragged her down to press his lips to hers. The mood shifted to one of greater urgency, and she let herself ride the sensation, closing her eyes as he reached down to stroke her, building the tension, coiling tighter and tighter until her vision blurred and she lost her breath, a voice that didn't even sound like hers calling out his name.

His fingers raked her back as he increased the tempo, and then his own climax overtook him and he crushed her to him, pumping hard, leaving her breathless and exhilarated. He held her tightly for a long moment, his breath harsh in her ears, then rolled to his side, taking her with him, his arms securely around her.

"How's your day now?" she asked, when she had

caught her breath. She traced one finger down his cheek, enjoying the roughness of his unshaved face.

"The best." He laid his head on her shoulder and closed his eyes. "The best."

"DYLAN, WAKE UP. Your phone is ringing."

Dylan opened his eyes and stared into Kayla's worried face. Still half asleep, he smiled and reached for her, but she pushed him away. "Your phone," she said. "Whoever it is has called back twice. You'd better answer it."

He struggled to sit, and wiped his hand over his eyes. He'd been deeply asleep, after an evening that had included the sandwich, a shower and another bout of lovemaking with Kayla before surrendering to slumber.

"Answer the phone." She nudged him.

He followed the sound of his ringtone to his trousers, which were on the floor atop his shirt and shoes. "Hello?" he croaked, then cleared his throat and tried again. "Hello?"

"There's been a development in the Matheson disappearance," Graham Ellison said. "Grand Junction Police found his car half submerged in an abandoned gravel pit. There was a bundle of bloody clothes shoved under the front seat. It looks like Daniel Metwater's prophecy might be true, after all."

Chapter Sixteen

Dylan met Graham and Simon at the Grand Junction impoundment yard a little after four in the morning. A forensics team was already at work on Matheson's car. Floodlights on tall stands illuminated the area around the vehicle, where technicians in white paper coveralls and booties combed the interior for hair and fibers, fingerprints, blood and any other evidence. Another man worked on the exterior, examining the body for recent dents and scratches, and collecting samples of soil from the tire treads.

"No good prints but a few of Matheson's own," Simon reported, after consulting with one of the techs. "They're sending the clothing to be tested to determine if the blood is Matheson's or someone else's."

"A dive team will search the gravel pit as soon as it's light," Graham said. "A second search team with cadaver dogs will comb the area around the pit."

"Any theories on what happened?" Dylan asked.
Graham shook his head. "A couple of kids ap-

parently drove out here to make out and noticed the top of the car in the moonlight," he said. "The girl mentioned it to her older sister when she got home, the sister told the dad and the dad called the police. They got a wrecker out here to haul it out of the water and when they ran the plate they knew they had something big."

"I think we should bring Metwater in for questioning," Simon said. "Maybe with this new development we can sweat a confession out of him."

"He's not going to break that easy," Dylan said. "And we don't have enough evidence to hold him. Until we have Matheson's body, we can't even charge him with murder. And he'll have a dozen followers who will swear he hasn't been anywhere near Grand Junction in months."

"Except Abe and Zach said they thought that's where he was for a big chunk of yesterday," Simon said.

"Which I'll admit makes him suspicious," Dylan said. "Except he supposedly had Andi Matheson with him, and considering her reaction to news that her father was dead, I can't imagine her conspiring with Metwater to kill the senator."

"Stranger things have happened," Simon said. "And if we don't detain him he's liable to disappear."

"We'll wait until we have a body," Graham said. "By then we may have enough evidence to make something stick. In the meantime, Michael and Marco are watching the camp. There's only one way into that canyon. The Prophet won't leave without our knowing it."

Simon pressed his lips together. Dylan knew he wasn't happy with this decision, but he wouldn't argue with their captain. Dylan sympathized with Simon's point of view. "Have you come up with anything in Metwater's background that we can use?" he asked. "I tried doing a little digging on my own, but you're better at background forensics than I am."

Simon shook his head. "We've got nothing. He's the blue blood heir to his family's manufacturing fortune. His dad died last year—apparently he'd had a heart condition for years and died on the operating table, so we can't blame that on the son. Metwater inherited equally with his twin brother, David, who was apparently the family screwup. He embezzled money from the family firm, got crosswise with some Mafia types and ended up dead. His body was found dumped in a river. He'd been shot in the head. A month later, Daniel declares he's had a spiritual revelation, sells the family business and takes his evangelical show on the road, recruiting followers to join his Family. And a few weeks ago they end up in our jurisdiction." He made a face. "Aren't we lucky?"

"So, no ties to the brother's death?"

"The local cops say he's clean. And it was pretty common knowledge that the brother was in over his head with organized crime."

"Maybe Daniel's religious conversion had more to do with fear the mob would come after him than a spiritual revelation," Graham said.

Simon shrugged. "If it did, he's taking it to extremes. If I had the fortune he has, I wouldn't be living in an RV in the middle of nowhere, without running water and electricity."

"When does their camping permit expire?" Dylan asked.

"Next week," Graham said. "But they can move to another spot in the wilderness area and renew the permit. For now, I would just as soon they stay put, where we can keep an eye on them."

They split up, Dylan and Simon in separate vehicles to head back to the Ranger Brigade offices, Graham to a meeting with FBI agents in the Bureau's Western Slope division. Dylan turned down his radio and contemplated the barren hills and red dirt washes that filled the landscape between Grand Junction and Montrose. He debated calling Kayla, to hear her voice and see how she was doing. Was she having any second thoughts about spending the night with him? Could he say anything to make her feel more comfortable with the decision?

Better to hold off on calling her. Right now it would be too easy for him to betray his own feelings and frighten her off. The truth was, he was falling in love with Kayla. Yes, it was happening fast, but he was as sure of his feelings as he had ever been sure of anything. He wouldn't take things too fast or try to push her, but he would find a way to gain her trust—to show her he was nothing like her father and the others who had let her down before.

He was almost to Montrose when his phone rang. "Lieutenant Holt?" a woman's voice asked hesitantly.

"Yes? Who is this?"

"This is Veronica Asher."

Dylan signaled and pulled to the side of the road. "How can I help you, Mrs. Asher?"

"I received something very strange in the mail this morning. I should probably call the Bureau, but frankly, I feel more comfortable talking to you."

"What did you receive?" he asked.

"It was a plain white envelope, addressed to Mrs. Frank Asher, with no return address, though the postmark is Grand Junction. Inside were a bunch of money cards—you know, the credit card things you can put a cash balance on. I called the number on the back of the cards and each one of them is worth twenty-five hundred dollars. Twenty-five thousand dollars in all."

"Twenty-five thousand dollars?" Dylan repeated. "Does that amount have any significance for you?"

"No. Except it's a crazy amount of money to get in the mail."

"Was there anything else in the envelope? A note?"

"There was a sympathy card, the kind you could buy in any store. No signature or anything."

"Do you know anyone in Grand Junction who might have sent you the money?" Dylan asked. "Maybe a charity or an organization that thought you needed the funds?"

"I don't know anyone in Grand Junction," she said. "And whatever his other faults, Frank left us well provided for. I don't know what to think about this except…" Her voice trailed away.

"Except what?"

"Do you think the money might be from Frank's killer? A kind of guilt payment or something?"

"That's definitely worth looking into. What have you done with the money cards?"

"Nothing. They're right here in the envelope they came in. But I wasn't being very careful at first. They'll have my fingerprints on them."

"Leave them there and call Frank's supervisor at the Bureau. They'll have the best resources to investigate this. Or I can contact them for you if you like."

"Would you? Every time I have to deal with them, all I can think is that they knew what Frank was up to and none of them bothered to tell me. That may be an unfair assessment, but it's how I feel."

"I'll call them and ask them to send over an agent—maybe someone who didn't work with Frank."

"Thank you."

She ended the call and Dylan mulled over the information she had given him. Daniel Metwater had a fortune at his disposal. It would have been easy enough for him to send one of his followers to one or more locations around Grand Junction to purchase the money cards with cash. He and Andi might even have purchased the cards themselves when they came to town yesterday. Even if Metwater hadn't personally pulled the trigger to kill Asher, he might have ordered one of his followers to do so. Maybe he had decided to alleviate some of his guilt by paying off Asher's widow.

Dylan put the Cruiser into gear and pulled back onto the highway. He would do as he had promised and notify the FBI of this latest development. But he would tell Graham first, and the Rangers would conduct an investigation of their own, one focused on Daniel Metwater and his followers.

KAYLA DRIFTED IN and out of sleep after Dylan left, her slumber disturbed by replays of their time together. While he had been with her, she had been sure a relationship with him was the best decision she had made in years. But away from his magnetic presence she felt less certain. She had been honest with him when she told him she didn't do relationships. She didn't have the emotional tools to be comfortable relying on someone else, and she had managed fine alone for years. He, on the other hand, was close to his family and more than comfortable with the idea of settling down with a wife and kids and the whole storybook setting. She didn't know how she would fit into that kind of life. Trying to make things work when they were so different was probably setting them both up for disappointment.

At seven she rose and made coffee, then switched on the television to the local morning program. "Very early today Grand Junction police recovered a vehicle belonging to missing senator Peter Matheson from an area gravel pit," the news anchor announced. "Divers are scheduled to search the pit for the body of the senator, who has been missing since last Friday." Video footage showed a late-model sedan being pulled from the water, the scene lit by floodlights. Superimposed on these images was a still photo of Senator Matheson, one Kayla recognized from his campaign posters.

Though Dylan had shared the news of the discovery before he had left for Ranger headquarters, seeing the footage on television somehow made it more real, Kayla found. She switched off the TV and returned to her bedroom to dress. She should have known news of the discovery of the senator's car would spread quickly. It was probably the top story on every channel. Even cut off from communication the way they were, Andi and the other Family members were bound to hear about this sooner rather than later. Dylan hadn't said, but Kayla suspected he or someone else from the Ranger Brigade would show up at the camp to question Daniel Metwater once more. Andi would be upset all over again. Kayla needed to be there for her.

She was on her way out the door when her phone rang. Hoping it was Dylan, she hurried to answer it, not even bothering to look at the screen.

"Hello, is this Kayla Larimer?"

"Yes." Kayla checked her phone. *Caller Unknown.* Had someone from the press gotten hold of her number?

"This is Madeline Zimeski, with the Colorado Private Investigators Society. I noticed we hadn't received your confirmation for the awards banquet this Thursday."

"I've been a little busy."

"So I can put down that you're coming? And how many guests?"

"Just me." She shifted her water bottle, digging in her purse for her car keys.

"You don't have someone you'd like to invite to see you receive your award?"

She thought of Dylan, then pushed the idea away. Why would he want to sit through a boring awards banquet? Besides, he had to attend Frank Asher's funeral. "Just me," she repeated. "And I really have to go now."

"I'll put you down for one then. Let me know if you change your mind about bringing a guest. I look forward to seeing you there. And congrat—"

Kayla ended the call and headed out the door to

her car. With luck she could make it to the camp before either Dylan or someone who had seen the television reports got there. She could break the news of this latest development to Andi gently and avoid sending the girl into tears yet again.

Traffic was light and she pushed the speed limit on her way out of town. She had just cleared the city limits when her phone rang again. A check of the screen showed an unknown number once more. If Madeline Zimeski had called back about that stupid awards banquet, she was going to get an earful.

Kayla was tempted not to answer, but what if it was Andi, calling from a pay phone? With one eye on the road, she took the call. "Hello?"

"Kayla? It's Pete Matheson. I need your help."

Chapter Seventeen

Kayla's car swerved and she almost dropped her phone. Heart pounding, she pulled over to the side of the road, leaving the engine idling. "Senator? Are you all right? Where are you? Are you hurt?"

"I'm not physically injured, but I need your help."

"Of course. Do you want me to call someone for you? Do you need money or someone to come get you?"

"Promise me you won't go to the authorities. Promise me now or I'll hang up and you'll never hear from me again."

"Of course. I promise. Don't hang up." Was someone there with him, telling him to say that? Did he have a gun to his head? What were the chances of Dylan and his team tracing this call?

"How is my daughter?"

The question was so conversational and unexpected that for a moment Kayla couldn't find the words to answer.

"You've seen her, haven't you?" the senator asked. "You told me you were going to see her."

"Uh, yes, I've seen her. She's well. Though she's very worried about you."

"Is she? I thought she might be glad to be rid of me."

"No! That isn't true. She was beside herself when she thought you were hurt. She loves you very much." The truth of those words made Kayla's chest hurt. Andi did love her father, no matter their differences.

He was silent for so long she thought he might have ended the call. "Senator? Are you still there?"

"I'm still here." He cleared his throat, and when he spoke his voice was rough with emotion. "I never meant to hurt her. You must believe that. Nothing I have is worth as much to me as my child."

"I believe Andi knows that. All she wants is for you to be safe."

"I need you to help me."

"To help you do what?"

"Can you take me to see Andi? Without anyone else knowing?"

"Why don't you want anyone else to know?" she asked. "So many people have been looking for you."

"No." His voice was sharp. "It's too dangerous at this point. When the time comes, I will notify the police. But not yet. Not until I've spoken with Andi."

"All right. I can do that." He wasn't really giving her a choice.

"I have an address for you, where you can pick me up. If you show up with any law enforcement, I'll go away and you won't hear from me again."

"I'll come alone, I promise," she said. "And I won't tell anyone where I'm going."

"Then get something to write this down. It will take you a while to get here, but I'll be waiting."

DYLAN TRIED TO reach Kayla, but her phone went straight to voice mail. Was she deliberately avoiding his calls? "Hey, Kayla, it's Dylan. I'm going to be out of touch for a while, on a stakeout. I'll call you when I'm back in cell range and maybe we can get together for dinner or something. Take care." He wanted to add something else—I miss you? I love you? But maybe it was too soon for that. He didn't want to scare her off. He settled for a simple "Bye" and stowed the phone once more.

Veronica Asher had scanned the money cards she had received and emailed the file to Simon, who was back at Ranger headquarters, combing through the identification numbers on the cards, trying to determine where they had originated from. Graham had made some calls to the FBI and the Bureau had promised to send a sympathetic agent to collect the cards from Mrs. Asher. They had agreed to work with the Rangers on canvassing Grand Junction area gas stations, convenience stores and grocery stores with pictures of as many of the Family members as they could obtain, in hopes of getting a positive ID on the purchaser of the cards. Once they had nailed that individual, they could use him or her to get to Daniel Metwater, or whoever had sent the cards.

The Rangers were also trying to get a warrant to access Metwater's bank records. A withdrawal in the amount of the payment to Mrs. Asher would be another strong indication of guilt. He might say he was only doing an anonymous good deed for the widow of the man who had been killed near his camp, but a prosecutor was likely to see things differently.

For now, Dylan was taking his shift watching the camp for any suspicious activity. He parked his Cruiser out of sight about a mile from Dead Horse Canyon and hiked to the rocky overlook DEA Agent Marco Cruz had selected as the best vantage point to survey the action in the compound without being seen.

"Anything going on?" Dylan asked Marco after the two had exchanged greetings.

"That big RV is Metwater's, right?" He handed over the high-powered binoculars he'd been using to surveil the camp. "He's had a lot of people going in and out of there—mostly women, but a few men. But I haven't seen him come out."

"How do we know he's still in there?" Dylan asked.

"No vehicles have left the camp, and Randall is

watching the road. If Metwater tried to climb out over the rocks we'd see."

Dylan settled more comfortably among the boulders and raised the binoculars. "Any sign of Andi Matheson?"

"She visited Metwater about an hour ago. When she came out it looked like she'd been crying. Any news on the senator?"

"Nothing yet. The FBI is canvassing the neighborhood near where they found the car, hoping to find a witness who saw something."

"It will be interesting to see whose blood is on those clothes," Marco said.

Dylan lowered the binoculars. "You don't think it's the senator's?"

Marco shrugged. "Who knows? It will just be interesting. One more piece of the puzzle." He stood and picked up his backpack. "I'm outta here."

"Hot date?"

He grinned. "You know it. Lauren is flying in from filming a documentary in Texas."

Dylan had forgotten that Cruz was married to television newscaster Lauren Starling. The two had met when she'd been kidnapped last summer and he'd been involved in her rescue. "I'm looking forward to meeting her soon," Dylan said. "Tell her I'm a fan."

"When I see her again, you are going to be the last thing on my mind."

Marco left, moving soundlessly down the rocks,

and Dylan settled back to watch. The summer days were growing shorter and here in the canyon the sun set quickly, plunging the area into darkness. As the air cooled and stars began to appear, activity increased in the camp. Dylan trained the binoculars on the center area, where two men were building a bonfire while a third man swept the dirt around the fire pit. About eight o'clock Metwater emerged from his trailer and walked over to supervise the preparations. Even at this distance, Dylan had a sense that something important was about to happen down there. Were they initiating another new member? Celebrating some religious rite he wasn't aware of? Throwing a birthday party?

He had a hard time picturing Metwater involved in something as innocent as a birthday party, but that was the kind of thing families did, wasn't it?

Metwater must have heard the news about Peter Matheson by now. Had Andi's tears when she left his trailer been because he had told her her father's car had been found in the quarry? Could whatever ceremony the group was preparing for have anything to do with the senator?

Carefully, Dylan moved a few feet farther down the slope, hoping for a better view of the action. He had no way of calling headquarters or summoning help without leaving his observation post and traveling back to the road. Better to see if he could figure out what was going on before he did that.

ANDI DROVE SLOWLY in the fading light, craning her head to read the addresses on the ramshackle buildings she passed. Her shoulders ached with tension, and her gun lay on the console beside her, loaded and ready. Everything about this setup felt like a trap to her. She wished now she had disobeyed the senator's orders and had at least let Dylan know where she was. He had tried to reach her shortly after she pulled onto the highway after talking with the senator, and she had let the call go to voice mail, knowing if she spoke to him directly she would give in to the temptation to share the news that Senator Matheson was alive and here in Montrose.

She hit the brakes as she spotted the address she wanted. She double-checked the number against the notes she had made, but this was the place. A faded sign identified the collection of boarded up buildings as the Shady Rest Motel. Judging by the prices on the gas pumps out front, this place hadn't been in business for at least a decade. Was someone holding the senator hostage here? She picked up the gun and climbed out of the car. "Senator Matheson!" she called, keeping her voice low.

"Hush. I'm right here."

She turned and saw him climbing into the passenger seat of her car. She might not have recognized him if she had passed him on the street. Instead of his usual tailored suit and tie, he wore a faded Hawaiian shirt and baggy khaki pants with a rip in the knee. He was unshaven and his hair needed combing. He looked more like a homeless person than a United States senator.

"Don't just stand there. Get in the car," he ordered.

The voice was the same at least, and the imperious tone. She slid back into the driver's seat, but kept her weapon at her side. "Senator, what happened to you?" she asked. "Are you all right?"

"I'm fine," he snapped, and fastened his seat belt.

"Do you need something to eat? Some water? Medical care?" She should have thought to bring him some food. She had a bottle of water and a first-aid kit, but if he needed more…

"I told you, I'm fine."

"The police found your car last night," she said.

"I heard on the news. I was hoping they wouldn't discover it for a while yet—that I'd have more time. Does Andi know?"

"I imagine she does by now." Surely someone would have reached the camp with the news.

"You said she was upset before. I imagine this won't calm her fears any."

"Daniel Metwater told her you were dead. He said he had a dream in which he saw your body covered in blood."

Matheson snorted. "Maybe he really is a prophet, after all." He leaned closer, studying her more intently. "What happened to your face?"

The bruises from her kidnappers' attack had faded

to a sickly yellow-purple and most of the swelling had subsided, though she still wouldn't win any beauty contests. "I was attacked while working a case," she said. Not exactly a lie.

"What case? Who hit you?"

She started to tell him that was none of his business, but she wanted to keep him talking. Eventually, she would work the conversation around to where he'd been and what he had been doing. "Two men attacked me outside Frank Asher's hotel room," she said. "They tried to kidnap me, but law enforcement intervened. One of the kidnappers was killed and the other one is in the hospital." Memory of the senator's connection with the event surfaced and it was her turn to scrutinize him. "Oddly enough, they were driving a van that was registered to you," she said. "A vehicle you used in your last campaign."

"None of that was supposed to happen," he said. "They were supposed to grab the laptop and any papers and leave. They weren't supposed to interfere with anyone or anything else."

She blinked, letting his words sink in. "Senator, are you saying those men were working for you? Under your orders?"

"I should have known better than to hire two petty criminals," he said. "I'm sorry you were injured. That should never have happened."

"Why did you hire them to steal Agent Asher's things?" she asked.

"I take protecting my daughter very seriously. I had to insure he didn't have anything incriminating in his possession."

"But, Senator—"

"Start the car." He motioned to the ignition. "We need to get out of here."

She turned the key. "Where are we going?"

"I want to see my daughter. I want you to take me to her."

"Do you want to stop and get something to eat first? Maybe a change of clothes?" Seeing her father like this was going to be a shock for Andi.

"No. I know what I look like. Now get going. We don't have any time to lose."

THE FAINT SCRAPE of a boot on the rocks above alerted Dylan that he wasn't alone. He turned to see Ethan Reynolds making his way toward him. "I came to relieve you," Ethan said. "Anything happening down there?" He jutted his chin toward the camp.

"They're building up the bonfire," Dylan said. "They're into rituals. I think they're getting ready for something like that."

"Cults use ritual to bond the members together," Ethan said. "They can also be useful in reinforcing the leader's message, applying peer pressure, even brainwashing."

"I forgot you were the cult expert."

Ethan settled more comfortably onto the rocks.

"I'm not sure this group qualifies as a full-fledged cult. The members seem to have autonomy, and the freedom to come and go."

"Yet none of them are leaving," Dylan said.

"Some of them may have nowhere else to go," Ethan said. "Groups like this tend to attract the disenfranchised."

"Andi Matheson has somewhere else to go, yet she's staying."

"She's found something she's looking for here."

"So what's your opinion of Metwater—twisted murderer or charismatic creep?"

Ethan shrugged. "Maybe neither. Maybe he's a sincere spiritual follower who rubs you the wrong way."

"Is that really what you think?"

"No. I'm voting for charismatic creep. He's slippery and manipulative and I think he's probably hiding something, but I can't see him pulling a trigger and blowing Agent Asher's head off. That's too emotional and visceral for him. He's a plotter, not a hothead."

"What about the money someone sent Asher's widow?"

"Maybe the money came from somewhere else."

"Where?"

"Maybe someone who read about the murder in the paper and felt sorry for the widow and three kids. Someone who wanted to remain anonymous."

"For the sake of our case, I hope it's not something that innocent."

"What about Andi Matheson?" Ethan asked. "Maybe she killed Asher because he left her high and dry with a baby."

"Maybe. But she seems even less likely than Metwater to kill a man in cold blood."

The fire below blazed up and Dylan shifted to look through the binoculars again. "Something happening?" Ethan asked.

A group of people had gathered around the fire, men and women in various stages of undress, their bodies painted, colored ribbons in their hair. As the flames leaped higher, they began to chant, the sound drifting up with the scent of piñon smoke in the clear night air.

"What are they saying?" Dylan asked. "I can't make it out."

"I think it's Latin," Ethan said.

Dylan lowered the binoculars. "You know Latin?"

He grinned. "I was a Catholic altar boy—but I've forgotten pretty much everything." He listened a moment. "I think it's something about sin. And maybe redemption or penance." He nodded. "Definitely penance in there."

Dylan raised the binoculars again. The door to the RV opened and Metwater emerged, dressed in the loincloth again, symbols traced in red and black and white paint on his chest and arms—circles and stars and arrows. They looked, Dylan decided, like a poor attempt at Native American imagery.

"Is that a dagger in that sheath at his waist?" Ethan had pulled out a second pair of binoculars and was focused on the scene below.

"It looks like the one I saw him with before," Dylan said.

"Maybe he's going to finish the ceremony you and Kayla interrupted the other night," Ethan said.

"Maybe." Or was he up to something more sinister?

Metwater clapped his hands over his head and the chanting ended midsyllable. When all eyes were on him he spoke, his voice loud and clear enough that Dylan could make out most of what he was saying. "We are assembled tonight to address the sin in our midst. We must break the chains of iniquity that bind us and purify our souls going forward."

"I'm not liking the sound of this," Dylan muttered. He could still picture the dark-haired girl with the blade to her throat, her eyes wide and terrified. Metwater could talk all he wanted about symbolic sacrifices, but it had all looked pretty real to Dylan.

Metwater motioned two men forward. They carried shovels and at his direction began shoveling coals from the fire and spreading them out in a wide path that led from the fire to Metwater's feet, some three yards away. Someone began drumming, a deep, steady rhythm like a heartbeat. Metwater addressed the crowd again, but the drumming made it impossible for Dylan to make out his words.

"I think he's telling them they're going to walk on the hot coals," Ethan said.

Dylan lowered the glasses once more to stare at him. "Seriously?"

"Fire walking has been practiced for thousands of years as a religious rite and a team-building exercise."

Dylan looked back to the camp. Metwater was motioning to the coals, while two women set basins of water at either end of the glowing path. "Now I know they're crazy," he said.

Ethan moved in beside him. "I've heard of this, but I've never seen it done before," he said. "Supposedly, the risk of injury is fairly minor, because the cool bottom of the foot does a good job of spreading out the heat, and the embers themselves actually don't conduct that much heat."

"That still doesn't make me want to walk barefoot over a bunch of hot coals," Dylan said.

"Who will be the first?" Metwater asked, his voice raised to carry over the drumming.

The silence from the group gathered around the fire was almost eerie.

"Asteria!" Metwater called. "Asteria, you shall be the first, to show us the way."

Andi stumbled forward, as if she had been pushed

from behind. Dylan tensed. "What does he think he's doing?" he asked. "She's pregnant."

Smiling, Metwater took Andi's hand and led her to the start of the fiery path, the coals glowing red against the darkness. "Don't do it," Dylan muttered.

Metwater knelt beside Andi and began to tie up her long skirts. She was trembling, the vibrations visible through Dylan's binoculars. He swore and stood. "I'm not going to let this happen," he said, and prepared to climb down the rocks. All he had to do was get within firing range.

With a loud cry, Andi whirled and fled into the darkness, leaving Metwater—and Dylan—staring after her.

Chapter Eighteen

Kayla let out the breath she'd been holding as Andi fled the fire-walking scene. Some of the tension went out of the senator's shoulders, too. "Thank God she hasn't lost all her senses," Matheson said. He turned away. "Come on, let's go find her. Now will be a good chance to talk to her without the others around."

He led the way around the camp. "You act as if you've been here before," Kayla said as she followed him.

"Only once. But I've got a good memory for details. Comes in handy in my job. Now if we keep traveling in this direction, we should be able to come up on the back of the camp. I'm guessing Andi would have fled to her quarters."

He sounded so sane and competent. A businessman with a job to do—such a contrast to his downtrodden appearance. On the drive over he had refused to answer Kayla's questions about what had happened to him and what he had been doing. He wouldn't deny or confirm that he had been kidnapped, and refused to discuss anything about his car or the clothes that had been found in it. "None of that is my concern right now," he said, in answer to all Kayla's queries.

As he had promised, the path they navigated led to the back of the camp. They could still hear chanting and shouts from the bonfire, but the noise was muffled by distance. Kayla wondered if anyone had taken Metwater up on his invitation to walk on hot coals. She noticed the Prophet hadn't volunteered to demonstrate how it was done.

"You'll have to show me which shelter is hers," Matheson said.

"The big tent, next to Metwater's RV." Kayla pointed to it. A lantern hung by the door, and a fainter glow emanated from within.

Matheson paused to draw himself up to his full height. "I'm ready," he said.

Before Kayla had time to react, he left the shadows where they had been hiding and strode the short distance to the tent. He entered without knocking or otherwise announcing himself. Kayla hurried after him and ducked inside in time to see Andi turn toward them, one hand to her throat. The young woman stared, mouth open, face ghostly pale.

Kayla hurried forward, afraid Andi would faint. "It's okay," she said, helping her to a low stool. "Your father wanted to see you."

"Daniel told me you were dead," Andi said, her gaze fixed on her father.

"Daniel was wrong." Matheson pulled another stool alongside his daughter. "I had to make sure you were okay," he said.

"I'm okay." She clutched his hands. "Better now that you're here. What happened, Daddy? I don't understand. Daniel said you were dead, and then we heard the police found your car, with bloody clothes inside."

"I had to go away for a while. And I will have to go away again soon." Matheson smoothed the hair back from her face. "I'm sorry I hurt you. The last thing I wanted to do was hurt you."

"You didn't hurt me," she said. "I'm okay, really."

"Frank Asher hurt you." Matheson grimaced. "I'm sorry I ever hired the man."

"Frank's gone now, Daddy. He's dead." Andi's lip trembled, but she regained her composure. "It doesn't matter. All that matters is that you're okay. I'm sorry. I'm sorry for all those terrible things I said to you. I just… I needed to live life my way, not your way."

"I know, honey, but you need to leave this place." He patted her hand. "That man—Daniel Metwater— he isn't good for you. What kind of man expects a pregnant woman to walk over hot coals? What is he trying to prove?"

"He wanted to free me from myself," Andi said. "He told me walking over the coals would burn away all my guilt and pain. But I wasn't brave enough. I didn't have enough faith."

It's not about faith, Kayla wanted to say. *It's about control.* But she bit back the words, not wanting to interrupt this moment between father and daughter.

"Come back home, Andi," Matheson said. "You'll be safe there. You can have your baby there and you'll never lack for anything. I have plenty of money put aside to make sure of that."

"My baby." She cradled her belly and her voice took on a crooning quality. "Poor baby. Her daddy's dead."

"Frank can't hurt you anymore," Matheson said. "I made sure of that."

Kayla started and moved closer. Andi stared at her father. "What do you mean?" she asked. "Someone killed Frank."

"I killed him," the senator said. "He told me he was coming here to see you again, to ask you not to make trouble for him over the baby. He wanted you to pretend he wasn't the father. He thought the affair would be bad for his career."

"You killed Frank?" Andi asked.

"I only intended to warn him off—to tell him to leave you alone. But he wouldn't listen. He was determined to see you. He'd already hurt you so much. I couldn't stand the thought of him hurting you again. I only meant to threaten him with the gun, but he wouldn't back down. I had to show him that I wouldn't back down, either. I had to protect you."

Kayla gasped. She hadn't even realized she'd made the noise until Matheson turned on her. "You weren't supposed to hear that," he said. "I was having a private conversation with my daughter."

"We all heard you, Senator." The tent flap lifted and Dylan stepped inside, followed by Ethan Reynolds. "Put your hands up and stand slowly," Dylan said. "Peter Matheson, I'm arresting you for the murder of Frank Asher."

"No." Matheson stood and backed up, until he bumped into Kayla. She was groping for her weapon when he grabbed her, his grip surprisingly strong. He wrenched the gun from her grasp and held it to her throat. "Don't come any closer or I'll kill her," he said. "You know I'll do it. I don't have anything to lose."

THE SIGHT OF that gun at Kayla's throat turned Dylan's blood to ice. He met her gaze, and the courage he saw behind her fear strengthened him. He holstered his weapon and took a step back, his hands out at his sides. "Take it easy," he told Matheson. "No one wants any trouble."

Ethan already had Andi and was ushering her out of the tent. Dylan trusted he would go for backup. Meanwhile, he had to find a way to deal with Matheson and save Kayla.

"You need to leave, too," Matheson said, one arm across Kayla's chest, the barrel of the gun pressed to her throat. "We're going to go away and you'll never see me again."

"You can go," Dylan said. "But leave Kayla behind. She hasn't done anything to hurt you."

"I'll let her go when I'm safely away from here."

"Where are you going to go?" Dylan asked. "You know if you leave, every cop in the country will be looking for you. If you give yourself up now, the courts will go easy on you. Any jury would understand a father wanting to protect his daughter."

"That's right. All I wanted to do was protect her. Asher laughed at me when I told him he didn't deserve her. Laughed!"

"He *didn't* deserve her," Dylan agreed. "And Kayla doesn't deserve to be involved in this. Let her go, Senator."

"I'm not a bad person," Matheson said. "I sent money to Asher's wife and kids, to try to make up for their loss. They're better off without him, too, I think."

"We know you're not a bad person," Dylan said. "Prove it by letting Kayla go."

"I won't hurt her," Matheson said. "I don't want to hurt anyone."

"I know you don't. Let her go."

Matheson no longer looked like the confident, determined man who had walked into the camp. He looked old and confused. Lost. "Where is Andi?" he asked. "Where's my girl?"

"She's safe, Senator," Dylan said. "But she's worried about you. She needs to know that you're safe, too. Haven't you put her through enough?"

"I only wanted to protect her." The barrel of the gun slid down, no longer pointed at Kayla's throat, though a shot at that close range would still be lethal. Kayla stiffened, and Dylan read the determination in her eyes.

Matheson seemed to gather himself also. "I'm leaving now," he said, some of the fog cleared from his expression. He took a step forward, tugging Kayla after him.

Kayla lunged forward, throwing all her weight into Matheson's back. He lost his balance and stumbled, and the gun went off, the bullet burying itself in the rug at his feet. Dylan pulled Kayla clear and shoved her behind him, then trained his gun on the senator, who lay sprawled on the floor. "Put your hands behind your head and don't move," Dylan ordered.

Matheson groaned, but did as commanded, and Ethan stepped in to cuff him. Once he was secure, Dylan holstered his weapon and turned to Kayla. "Are you all right?" he asked.

"I'm fine." She was pale and her voice shook, but her eyes were clear and steady. "You showed up just in time."

He pulled her close and cradled her face against his chest, shaky with relief now that the danger was past. "We were doing surveillance on the camp and saw you arrive with Matheson," he said.

"Did you know he had killed Agent Asher?"

"No. But I imagine the lab reports on Matheson's clothes will show the blood is Frank Asher's," Dylan said. "He must have sunk the car himself to hide that evidence."

"When I picked him up this evening he told me he had hoped it would take police longer to find the car—that he'd have more time. Time for what?"

"To figure out how to get out of the country? To prepare to turn himself in?" Dylan shook his head. "Who knows?"

Kayla turned to watch Ethan lead Matheson away. "I feel sorry for him," she said. "I think he blamed Asher for his own estrangement from Andi."

"Killing the man didn't solve anything."

"I know, but love can make people do the wrong thing for the right reasons."

Dylan pulled her more tightly against him. "I think my heart stopped for a second when I saw you with that gun to your throat," he said. "All I could think of was that if I couldn't stop him from hurting you, I wouldn't be able to live with myself."

She looked up at him. "I don't need a man to rescue me. Just one to be there alongside me."

"I'm starting to figure that out."

"Then you're starting to understand me," she said.

"I don't have to understand you," he said. "I just want to be with you."

"That's a good place to start." She slid one hand to the back of his head and pulled his mouth down to hers. The kiss, more than her words, told him everything was going to be all right between them. They'd found Frank Asher's killer. Kayla was safe. And they would figure out a way to meld her need for independence with his need to protect. Life wasn't a fairy tale, but he still believed in happy endings.

Epilogue

"Do I look all right?" Kayla tugged at the skirt of the dress she had chosen for the awards banquet and frowned at her reflection in the mirror. "I hate this stuff. You know that, don't you?"

Madeline Zimeski, president of the Colorado Private Investigators Society, patted Kayla's back. "You look lovely, dear. I'm only sorry your family couldn't be here to see you receive your award."

"They live out of state," Kayla said. It was easier than explaining the truth—that she didn't have any family who cared enough about her to walk across the street, much less attend an awards banquet.

Madeline checked her cell phone. "It's almost time for the awards," she said. "We'd better get back." Kayla had been hiding in the ladies' room when Madeline had come in search of her. Clearly, the president wasn't going to let even one honoree escape her moment in the spotlight.

Reluctantly, Kayla followed her back to the front table where she had been seated, her back to most of the crowd. She'd managed to choke down a few bites of dinner and make polite small talk with the board members and other honorees at her table, and was counting the minutes until she'd be free to leave.

Madeline strode to the podium and made a show of adjusting the microphone. "Now is the point in the program I know we've all been waiting for," she said. "Our annual awards. Each year we honor those of our members we feel are the finest representatives of our craft." She droned on about the voting process, the history of the organization and some other things Kayla couldn't focus on. She squirmed in her chair and wished she had opted for a drink from the bar.

"And first up, our senior private detective of the year, Malcolm Stack."

A tall man with a shock of white hair walked to the podium to accept the plaque Madeline handed him. Kayla stared at her water glass, mentally rehearsing the brief thank-you she planned to deliver.

"And for our Western Slope PI of the year, Kayla Larimer."

She had expected Madeline to draw out the ceremony more, so the announcement of her name caught her off guard. Awkwardly, she shoved back her chair and stood as a smattering of applause rose around her. As she started toward the podium a chorus of shouts and whistles echoed from the back of the room. Startled, she whirled to see Dylan standing at a table near the back. Beside him, his mother and father stood also, both clapping wildly.

"Kayla?" Madeline prompted from the podium.

Flustered, Kayla made her way to the stage. Madeline shoved the plaque into her hand, and a flash almost blinded her. "Say something," Madeline hissed, and nudged her toward the microphone.

"Umm…" Kayla stared at the plaque. Nervous laughter rose from a few people near the front. She cleared her throat and fought for composure. "Thank you for this honor," she said. She looked out across the room and caught Dylan's eyes. He was grinning like a fool, and gave her a thumbs-up. She couldn't help but smile. "And thank you to all the people who have helped me along the way. And to those who continue to support me now."

She managed to make it down the steps from the dais without tripping, but instead of returning to her chair, she walked the length of the room to join Dylan and his parents.

"Congratulations," Bud Holt said, and pumped her hand.

"We're so proud of you," Nancy added, and patted her arm.

Kayla looked at Dylan. "What are you doing here?" she asked. "Aren't you supposed to be at a funeral?"

"You didn't think I was going to pass up the chance to see you honored like this, did you?" He hugged her to him.

"I guess you don't really need to go to Frank Asher's funeral now that the case is closed," she said.

"Even if it was still open, I wouldn't miss your big night," he said.

She held out the plaque and read the text, which proclaimed her as the Western Slope Private Investigator of the Year. "It's not such a big deal."

"It is to me." He kissed the top of her head. "I'm proud of you," he said. "You deserve this."

She turned to his parents. "I can't believe you came," she said. "Thank you so much."

"You're special to Dylan, so you're special to us, too," Nancy said. "Congratulations." She nudged her husband. "Now, I think we should leave these two alone."

They left and Dylan led Kayla into the hallway. "Senator Matheson agreed to a plea deal today," he said.

"I guess that's for the best," she said. "How much time will he serve?"

"He pleaded involuntary manslaughter. He could be out as soon as eighteen months."

"What about Andi?"

"She wants to stay with Metwater and his bunch. She says she feels at home there."

"I guess Daniel Metwater was innocent, after all."

"Of murder. I still think he's up to something." Dylan pushed open the door to the parking lot. "We'll be keeping a close eye on him, as long as he's in our jurisdiction."

"I plan to stay in touch with Andi, too," Kayla said. "It's funny, when you think about it, how the two of us hit it off."

"Not so strange, really. You both are independent women and felt you didn't fit in with your family's lifestyle."

"I guess that's one way to look at it."

"Were you surprised to see us tonight?" he asked.

"I can't think of when I've been more surprised." She stopped at the edge of the covered walkway that led up to the building and turned to him. "Am I really special to you?"

"You didn't know that already?"

She pressed her palm against his chest. "I guess I did, but I wanted to be sure."

"I love you," he said. "Did you know that?"

"I love you, too. And it scares me. I've never allowed myself to love this much before."

"Don't be afraid." He pulled her to him. "You can count on me, Kayla Larimer. I'm promising here and now that I'm always going to protect you and care for you and do my best for you."

"You know the best thing about all of that?" she asked.

"What?"

"I believe you. And I'm going to do the same for you, Dylan Holt."

"That's what matters most, isn't it?" he said. "Knowing we can count on each other."

"Mmm." She pulled his face down to hers. "Less talking, more kissing."

"Yes, ma—mmm."

* * * * *

THE RANGER BRIGADE: FAMILY SECRETS
miniseries is just getting started.
*Don't miss the next book from Cindi Myers when
it goes on sale in July 2017.*

*Look for it wherever
Harlequin Intrigue books are sold!*

Want more Cindi Myers? Check out
THE MEN OF SEARCH TEAM SEVEN:

*COLORADO CRIME SCENE
LAWMAN ON THE HUNT
CHRISTMAS KIDNAPPING
PHD PROTECTOR*

Available now from Harlequin Intrigue!

DARBY CAHILL ADJUSTED his Stetson as he moved toward the bandstand. The streets of Gilt Edge, Montana, were filled with revelers who'd come to celebrate the yearly chokecherry harvest on this beautiful day. The main street had been blocked off for all the events. People had come from miles around for the celebration of a cherry that was so tart it made your mouth pucker.

As he climbed the steps, Darby figured it just proved that people would celebrate anything. Normally, his twin sister, Lillie, attended, but this year she was determined that he should do more of their promotion at these events.

"I hate it as much as you do," she'd assured him. "But believe me, you'll get more attention up there on the stage than me. Just say a few words, throw T-shirts into the crowd, have some fry bread and come home. You can do this." Clearly, she knew his weakness for fry bread as well as his dislike of being the center of attention.

The T-shirts were from the Stagecoach Saloon, the bar and café the two of them owned and operated outside town. Since it had opened, the bar had helped sponsor the Chokecherry Festival each year.

He heard his name being announced and sighed as he made his way up the rest of the steps to the microphone to deafening applause. He tipped his hat to the crowd, swallowed the lump in his throat and said, "It's an honor to be here and to be part of such a wonderful celebration."

"Are you taking part in the pit-spitting competition?" someone yelled from the crowd, and others joined in. Along with being bitter, chokecherries were mostly pit.

"I'm going to leave that to the professionals," he said, reaching for the box of T-shirts, wanting this over with as quickly as possible. He didn't like being in the spotlight any longer than he had to. Also, he hoped that once he started throwing the shirts, everyone would forget about the pit-spitting contest later.

He was midthrow when he spotted a woman in the crowd. What had caught his eye was the brightly colored scarf around her dark hair. It fluttered in the breeze, giving him glimpses of only her face.

He let go and the T-shirt sailed through the air as if caught on the breeze. He saw with a curse that it was headed right for the woman. Grimacing, he watched the rolled up T-shirt clip the woman's shoulder.

She looked up, clearly startled. He had the impression of serious, dark eyes, full lips. Their gazes locked for an instant and he felt something like lightning pierce his heart. For a moment, he couldn't breathe. Rooted to the spot, all he could hear was the drumming of his heart, the roaring crowd a dull hum in the background.

Someone behind the woman in the crowd scooped up the T-shirt and, scarf fluttering, the woman turned away, disappearing into the throng of people.

What had *that* been about? His heart was still pounding. What had he seen in those bottomless dark eyes that left him...breathless? He knew what Lillie would have said. Love at first sight. Something he would have scoffed at—just moments ago.

"Do you want me to help you?" a voice asked at his side.

Darby nodded to the festival volunteer. He threw another T-shirt, looking in the crowd for the woman. She was gone.

Once the box of T-shirts was empty, he hurriedly stepped off the stage into the moving mass. His job was done. His plan was to have some fry bread and then head back to the saloon. He was happiest behind the bar. Or on the back of a horse. Being Montana born and raised in open country, crowds made him nervous.

The main street had been blocked off and now booths lined both sides of the street all the way up the hill that led out of town. Everywhere he looked there were chokecherry T-shirts and hats, dish towels and coffee mugs. Most chokecherries found their way into wine or syrup or jelly, but today he could have purchased the berries in lemonade or pastries or even barbecue sauce. He passed stands of fresh fruit and vegetables, crafts of all kinds and every kind of food.

As he moved through the swarm of bodies now filling the downtown street, the scent of fry bread in the air, he couldn't help searching for the woman. That had been the strangest experience he'd ever had. He told himself it could have been heatstroke had the day been hotter. Also, he felt perfectly fine now.

He didn't want to make more of it than it was, and yet, he'd give anything to see her again. As crazy as it sounded, he couldn't throw off the memory of that sharp hard shot to his heart when their gazes had met.

As he worked his way through the crowd, following the smell of fry bread, he watched for the colorful scarf the woman had been wearing. He needed to know what that was about earlier. He told himself he was being ridiculous, but if he got a chance to see her again...

Someone in the crowd stumbled against his back. He caught what smelled like lemons in the air as a figure started to brush by him. Out of the corner of his eye, he saw the colorful scarf wrapped around her head of dark hair.

Like a man sleepwalking, he grabbed for the end of the scarf as it fluttered in the breeze. His fingers closed on the silken fabric, but only for a second. She was moving fast enough that his fingers lost purchase and dropped to her arm.

In midstep, she half turned toward him, his sudden touch slowing her. In those few seconds, he saw her face, saw her startled expression. He had the bizarre thought that this woman was in trouble. Without realizing it, he tightened his grip on her arm.

Her eyes widened in alarm. It all happened in a manner of seconds. As she tried to pull away, his hand slid down the silky smooth skin of her forearm until it caught on the wide bracelet she was wearing on her right wrist.

Something dropped from her hand as she jerked free of his hold. He heard a snap and her bracelet came off in his hand. His gaze went to the thump of whatever she'd dropped as it hit the ground. Looking down, he saw what she'd dropped. *His wallet?*

Astonishment rocketed through him as he realized that when she'd bumped into him from behind, she'd picked his pocket! Feeling like a fool, he bent to retrieve his wallet. Jostled by the meandering throng, he quickly rose and tried to find her, although he wasn't sure what exactly he planned to do when he did. Music blared from a Western band over the roar of voices.

He stood holding the woman's bracelet in one

hand and his wallet in the other, looking for the bright scarf in the mass of gyrating festivalgoers.

She was gone.

Darby stared down at his wallet, then at the strange, large, gold-tinted cuff bracelet and laughed at his own foolishness. His moment of "love at first sight" had been with a *thief*? A two-bit pickpocket? Wouldn't his family love this!

Just his luck, he thought as he pocketed his wallet and considered what to do with what appeared to be heavy, cheap, costume jewelry. He'd been lucky. He'd gotten off easy in more ways than one. His first thought was to chuck the bracelet into the nearest trash can and put the whole episode behind him.

But he couldn't quite shake the feeling he'd gotten when he'd looked into her eyes—or when he'd realized the woman was a thief. Telling himself it wouldn't hurt to keep a reminder of his close call, he slipped the bracelet into his jacket pocket.

MARIAH AYERS GRABBED her bare wrist, the heat of the man's touch still tingling there. What wasn't there was her prized bracelet, she realized with a start. Her heart dropped. She hadn't taken the bracelet off since her grandmother had put it on her, making her promise never to part with it.

This will keep you safe and bring you luck, Grandmother Loveridge had promised on her deathbed. *Be true to who you are.*

She fought the urge to turn around in the surging throng of people, go find him and demand he give it back. But she knew she couldn't do that for fear of being arrested. Or worse. So much for the bracelet bringing her luck, she thought, heart heavy. She had no choice but to continue moving as she was swept up in the flowing crowd. Maybe she could find a high spot where she could spot her mark. And then what?

Mariah figured she'd cross that bridge when she came to it. Pulling off her scarf, she shoved it into her pocket. It was a great device for misdirection—normally—but now it would be a dead giveaway.

Ahead, she spotted stairs and quickly climbed half a dozen steps at the front of a bank to stop and look back.

The street was a sea of cowboy hats. One cowboy looked like another to her. How would she ever be able to find him—let alone get her bracelet back given that by now he would know what she'd been up to? She hadn't even gotten a good look at him. Shaken and disheartened, she told herself she would do whatever it took. She desperately needed that bracelet back—and not just for luck or sentimental reasons. It was her ace in the hole.

Two teenagers passed, arguing over which one of them got the free T-shirt they'd scored. She thought of the cowboy she'd seen earlier up on the stage, the one throwing the T-shirts. He'd looked right at her.

Their gazes had met and she'd felt as if he had seen into her dark heart—if not her soul.

No wonder she'd blown a simple pick. She was rusty at this, clearly, but there had been a time when she could recall each of her marks with clarity. She closed her eyes. Nothing. Squeezing them tighter, she concentrated.

With a start, she recalled that his cowboy hat had been a light gray. She focused on her mark's other physical attributes. Long legs clad in denim, slim hips, muscular thighs, broad shoulders. A very nice behind. She shook off that image. A jean jacket over a pale blue checked shirt. Her pickpocketing might not be up to par, but at least there was nothing wrong with her memory, she thought as she opened her eyes and again scanned the crowd. Her uncle had taught her well.

But she needed more. She closed her eyes again. She'd gotten only a glimpse of his face when he'd grabbed first her scarf and then her arm. Her eyes flew open as she had a thought. He must have been on to to her immediately. Had she botched the pick that badly? She really *was* out of practice.

She closed her eyes again and tried to concentrate over the sound of the two teens still arguing over the T-shirt. Yes, she'd seen his face. A handsome, rugged face and pale eyes. Not blue. No. Gray? Yes. With a start she realized where she'd seen him before. It was the man from the bandstand, the one who'd thrown the T-shirt and hit her. She was sure of it.

"Excuse me, I'll buy that T-shirt from you," she said, catching up to the two teens as they took their squabble off toward a burger stand.

They both turned to look at her in surprise. "It's not for sale," said one.

The other asked, "How much?"

"Ten bucks."

"No way."

"You got it for *free*," Mariah pointed out, only to have both girls' faces freeze in stubborn determination.

"Fine, twenty."

"Make it thirty," the greedier of the two said.

She shook her head as she dug out the money. Her grandmother would have given them the evil eye. Or threatened to put some kind of curse on them. "You're thieves, you know that?" she said as she grabbed the T-shirt before they could take off with it *and* her money.

Escaping down one of the side streets, she finally got a good look at what was printed across the front of the T-shirt. Stagecoach Saloon, Gilt Edge, Montana.

LILLIE CAHILL HESITATED at the back door of the Stagecoach Saloon. It had been a stagecoach stop back in the 1800s when gold had been coming out of the mine at Gilt Edge. Each stone in the saloon's walls,

like each of the old wooden floorboards inside, had
a story. She'd often wished the building could talk.

When the old stagecoach stop had come on the
market, she had jumped at purchasing it, determined
to save the historical two-story stone building. It had
been her twin's idea to open a bar and café. She'd
been skeptical at first, but trusted Darby's instincts.
The place had taken off.

Lately, she felt sad just looking at the place.

Until recently, she'd lived upstairs in the remod-
eled apartment. She'd moved in when they bought
the old building and had made it hers by collecting
a mix of furnishings from garage sales and junk
shops. This had not just been her home. It was her
heart, she thought, eyes misting as she remembered
the day she'd moved out.

Since her engagement to Trask Beaumont and the
completion of their home on the ranch, she'd given up
her apartment to her twin, Darby. He had been living in a cabin not far from the bar, but he'd jumped
at the chance to live upstairs.

Now she glanced toward the back window. The
curtains were some she'd left when she'd moved out.
One of them flapped in the wind. Darby must have
left the window open. She hadn't been up there to see
what he'd done with the place. She wasn't sure she
wanted to know, since she'd moved most everything
out, leaving it pretty much a blank slate. She thought
it might still be a blank slate, knowing her brother.

Pushing open the back door into the bar kitchen, she was met with the most wonderful of familiar scents. Fortunately, not everything had changed in her life, she thought, her mood picking up some as she entered the warm café kitchen.

"Tell me those are your famous enchiladas," she said to Billie Dee, their heavyset, fiftysomething Texas cook.

"You know it, sugar," the cook said with a laugh. "You want me to dish you up a plate? I've got home-made pinto beans and some Spanish rice like you've never tasted."

"You mean *hotter* than I've ever tasted."

"Oh, you Montanans. I'll toughen you up yet."

Lillie laughed. "I'd love a plate." She pulled out a chair at the table where the help usually ate in the kitchen and watched Billie Dee fill two plates.

"So how are the wedding plans coming along?" the cook asked as she joined her at the table.

"I thought a simple wedding here with family and friends would be a cinch," Lillie said as she took a bite of the enchilada. She closed her eyes for a moment, savoring the sweet and then hot bite of peppers before all the other flavors hit her. She groaned softly. "These are the best you've ever made."

"Bless your heart," Billie Dee said, smiling. "I take it the wedding has gotten more complicated?"

"I can't get married without my father and who knows when he'll be coming out of the mountains."

Their father, Ely Cahill, was a true mountain man now who spent most of the year up in the mountains either panning for gold or living off the land. He'd given up ranching after their mother had died and had turned the business over to her brothers Hawk and Cyrus.

Their oldest brother, Tucker, had taken off at eighteen. They hadn't seen or heard from him since. Their father was the only one who wasn't worried about him.

Tuck needs space. He's gone off to find himself. He'll come home when he's ready, Ely had said.

The rest of the family hadn't been so convinced. But if Tuck was anything like their father, they would have heard something from the cops. Ely had a bad habit of coming out of the mountains thirsty for whiskey—and ending up in their brother Sheriff Flint Cahill's jail. Who knew where Tuck was. Lillie didn't worry about him. She had four other brothers to deal with right here in Gilt Edge.

"I can see somethin's botherin' you," Billie Dee said now.

Lillie nodded. "Trask insists we wait to get married since he hopes to have the finishing touches on the house so we can have the reception there."

Trask, the only man she'd ever loved, had come back into her life after so many years that she'd thought she'd never see him again. But they'd found their way back together and now he was building a house for them on the ranch he'd bought not far from the bar.

"Waitin' sounds reasonable," the cook said between bites.

"I wish we'd eloped."

"Something tells me the wedding isn't the problem," Billie Dee said, using her fork to punctuate her words.

"I'll admit it's been hard giving up my apartment upstairs. I put so much love into it."

"Darby will take good care of it."

Don't miss
OUTLAW'S HONOR,
available June 2017 wherever
HQN Books and ebooks are sold.

www.Harlequin.com

INTRIGUE

*Madison Goode knows just the man for the job to stop
a cybersecurity breach at an art museum reception—
but why is he on the guest list as her husband?*

*Read on for a sneak preview of
MARRIAGE CONFIDENTIAL,
by USA TODAY bestselling authors
Debra Webb and Regan Black!*

She glanced up and down the hallway before meeting
his gaze. "Spend a few minutes at the reception with
me. News of my, um, husband's arrival has made people
curious."

He kept her waiting, but she didn't flinch. "Okay, on
one condition."

"Only one?"

He reconsidered his position. "One condition and I
reserve the right to add conditions based on your answers."

She held her ground and his gaze. "I reserve the right to
refuse on a per item basis. Name your primary condition."

He felt the smile curl his lips, saw her lovely mouth
curve in reply. "Tell me where and why we married."

"Not here." Her smile faded. "You deserve a full
explanation and you'll get it, I promise. As soon as I
navigate the minefield this evening has become. I don't
have any right to impose further, but I could use a buffer
in there."

He suddenly wanted to step up and be that buffer. For her. "I'm no asset in social settings, Madison."

"No one's expecting you to be a social butterfly. You only have to be yourself and pretend to be proud of me."

He didn't care for her phrasing. Before he could debate the terms further, she leaned her body close to his and gave him a winning smile. "Later," she murmured, tapping his lips with her finger. "Let's go. There's only an hour left." She linked her hand with his and turned, giving a start when they came face-to-face with one of the guests.

Her moves made sense now. She'd known they were being watched while he'd been mesmerized by her soft green eyes. The intimacy had only been for show. Thank goodness.

The only thing that came naturally to him was demonstrating pride in his fake wife. She had a flare for diplomacy—no surprise, considering her career. He admired her ability to say the right things or politely evade questions she didn't want to answer.

When they entered the gallery where the prized white jade cup glowed under soft lights surrounded by guards, he was the only person close enough to catch her relieved sigh. She squeezed his hand. "Thank you, Sam. You saved me tonight."

Don't miss
MARRIAGE CONFIDENTIAL,
available July 2017 wherever
Harlequin® Intrigue books and ebooks are sold.

www.Harlequin.com

HIEXP0617

EXCLUSIVE LIMITED TIME OFFER AT
www.HARLEQUIN.com

New York Times Bestselling Author
B.J. DANIELS
OUTLAW'S HONOR

She never expected this Cahill to be her hero—or the only man she'd need.

Available May 30, 2017.
Get your copy today!

$1.⁰⁰ OFF

$7.99 U.S./$9.99 CAN.

Receive **$1.00 OFF** the purchase price of
OUTLAW'S HONOR by B.J. Daniels
when you use the coupon code below on Harlequin.com.

OUTLAW1

Offer valid from May 30, 2017, until June 30, 2017, on www.Harlequin.com.
Valid in the U.S.A. and Canada only. To redeem this offer, please add the print or ebook version of OUTLAW'S HONOR by B.J. Daniels to your shopping cart and then enter the coupon code at checkout.

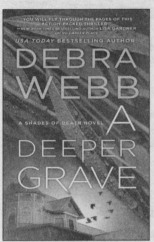